HE SAW JESUS

Jesus' Joy

To Girlinde,

HE SAW JESUS

Jesus' Joy

May you know his joy,

BETTY ARRIGOTTI

Betty Arrigotti

DEDICATION

To everyone who struggles because they are atypical. May they discover the beautiful variety their uniqueness brings to life.

Prologue

Bernard Lovejoy stared at the results from the DNA test he'd taken. At forty, he told himself, he should be content with who he was and not need more. Yet, he'd always felt that his parents hadn't told him something. He didn't look like either of them, both olive-skinned brunettes. Not another relative that he'd met had his fair complexion and red hair. His personality was unlike his father's or his mother's. They had never talked about when his mom was pregnant with him, or whether his birth was difficult. But he loved his parents and didn't want to upset them, so he had pushed his questions and doubts aside. They had a happy life. He was a good son, visiting them often once he'd become a teacher and moved out, and caring for their needs as they aged.

Then they had both passed this year, only a few months apart, in their early 70s. At the second funeral—his mother's—an elderly aunt took his hand as she was leaving and casually said, "You were such a blessing to your parents when you were given to them."

Stunned, he murmured his thanks, and then she was gone without answering the confusing questions she had raised in his mind. *When you were given to them?* Did she mean when God blessed them with a child? Or was he someone else's child, and he was given to them? Was he adopted? That's why he'd done a DNA test a few weeks ago, and now the results were in his hands, raising more questions still.

He read that he had a half-brother, named Daniel Roma, born the year before him.

Half? Was it his mother or his father who had a child he'd never heard about? And Roma? Whose name was that? It must have been his mother who also mothered Daniel, or they'd share their father's surname. Or was he not blood-related to either of his parents? He knew they had been married several years before he was born. He couldn't imagine either of his parents being untrue to the other. He must have been adopted!

Bernard knew that he sometimes harbored obsessive tendencies. This new information would not be something he could ignore. With only a few weeks left of the school year, he'd need to force himself to be patient. When summer break came, he could travel and search and perhaps find answers to the mystery of his birth. But between now and then, he knew every spare thought would be focused on researching his brother.

HE SAW JESUS

jerked		jit'ney		jol'li·er	
jerk'i·ly		jit'ters		jol'li·est	
jer'kin		jit'ter·y		jol'li·fi·ca'tion	
jerk'y		job		jol'li·ty	
jer'sey		job'ber		jol'ly	
jest		jock'ey		jolt	
jest'er		jo·cose'		jolt'ed	
jest'ing·ly		jo·cose'ly		jon'quil	
Jes'u·it		jo·cos'i·ty		jos'tle	
Je'sus		joc'u·lar		jos'tled	
jet		joc'u·lar'i·ty		jot	
jet'sam		joc'u·lar·ly		jot'ted	
jet'ti·son		joc'und		jounce	
jet'ty		jo·cun'di·ty		jour'nal	
jew'el		jodh'purs		jour'nal·ism	
jew'eled		jog		jour'nal·ist	
jew'el·er		jogged		jour'nal·is'tic	
jew'el·ry		jog'gle		jour'nal·ize	
Jew'ish		jog'gled		jour'nal·ized	
Jew'ry		join		jour'ney	
jibe		join'der		jour'neyed	
jig		joined		jour'ney·man	
jig'ger		join'er		jo'vi·al	
jig'gle		join'ings		jo'vi·al'i·ty	
jig'gled		joint		jo'vi·al·ly	
jig'saw'		joint'ed		jowl	
jin'gle		joint'ly		joy	
jin'gled		join'ture		joy'ful	
jin'go		joist		joy'ful·ly	
jin'go·ism		joke		joy'ful·ness	
jin·rik'i·sha		jok'er		joy'less	
jinx		jok'ing·ly		joy'ous	

Gregg Shorthand Dictionary, Miniature, Gregg, John Robert, Leslie, Louis A, Zoubek, Charles E. McGraw-Hill Book Company, copyright 1963, p. 158.

Chapter 1

Her name was Pedra Clump. Not a pretty name like Clarissa or Katerina or Melanie, but she guessed it fit. She wasn't a pretty woman. She also couldn't claim to be very clever, coordinated, creative, or classy. Yet, she did one thing well. She took dictation fast with surprisingly accurate shorthand. So, she had become a secretary and supported herself adequately for the first ten years of her adult life. However, with the coming of computers and smart phones, there didn't seem to be much use for shorthand. Bosses could speak and see their words typed out. Or they left messages or texts. Little by little, her one skill became archaic. So, three months ago, after not having a single date since high school, she decided to become a nun.

She picked a nursing order since it was closest to where she lived. Even she admitted her decision was not exactly clever. Put to work as an aide, she discovered she didn't do well with blood or bodily fluids or seeing people in pain. She did, however, like visiting with the patients, which often landed her in trouble for wasting time. She hoped she could remain an aide, if not a nurse, but over time she suspected they were going to send her home, having failed as a postulant.

However, one day, that all changed.

That morning, Bishop Raymond visited one of the patients in the rehabilitation wing of the hospital, and then conferred with the Reverend Mother, who was in charge of the nurses. He asked her to have someone write down the patient's stories, and the job fell to Pedra. She brightened at the idea and hoped she could prove herself useful.

That afternoon, dressed in her usual black jumper and white blouse, Pedra entered the patient's room. His chart just said Frank, no last name. *Maybe he has an ugly last name, too,* she thought. He was lying in the hospital bed, not making a very large lump under the covers. His face was pale, almost grey enough to match his hair. He looked to be in his late 60s, yet his blue eyes were full of life, and he smiled broadly. Pedra introduced herself and told him she'd like to visit him and hear some of his stories.

"Bishop Raymond's orders?" he asked.

"And Mother Superior's," she admitted.

"Well, we both have promised to be obedient. I guess we should begin. But where to start?"

"The bishop said to ask you about your First Communion."

"Yes, I suppose it does begin there."

She settled into the chair next to him with a steno pad and a sharp pencil, and he began to tell her the story of his life.

∞

When I was seven, I woke one night with a start. A strange woman stood at the foot of my bed. She smiled at me, and then I wasn't afraid. Such a sweet smile couldn't mean anyone any harm. A blue scarf covered most of her hair, and she wore a blue top and white pants, all very loose and flowy.

"Frank," she said.

I nodded, still not quite convinced this was real, and yet wondered whether this was a stranger I wasn't supposed to talk to.

"Frank, you are a lucky boy. Very blessed. You will see my son Jesus soon! He won't look like you expect, but know He loves you very much."
Then I blinked, and she was gone. I looked all around my little room but didn't see her anywhere. How did she disappear so fast?

I blinked again and decided I had dreamed it, though I didn't feel any more awake than I had before. I felt a little sad because she appeared so beautiful and kind. I would have liked to talk to her more. Yes, I decided, I had been happier when she was in my room, and now the room and my heart both felt emptier.

Pushing back the covers, I got up and opened my door to peek out into the hallway. She wasn't there, which made sense since I hadn't seen or heard the door open. I looked under my bed and in my closet, but she wasn't there either. It was a small room, with nowhere else to hide.

I sat on my bed and tried to remember everything she said. "You are a lucky boy. Very blessed. You will see my son Jesus soon. He won't look like you expect." There was something else. Oh! "He loves you very much." What did she mean, soon? This was definitely a mama question. I found my mother in the kitchen, getting our lunches ready for the next day. I remember the aroma of bacon and being pleased because she was making my favorite sandwiches. I told her what had happened.

Mama was a calm person, not upset very easily, but she looked worried, or maybe scared. "You must have had a very realistic dream," she said.

"Maybe," I answered. "It seemed so real, and I was sad when she was gone."

Mama took me to the living room and pulled me onto her lap on the old brown couch. "Tell me about it again," she said, and I did. While I talked, her face drained color to whiter than her usual rosy pink. She definitely looked scared. She had looked that way once before when I fell and needed stitches. But why now?

It began to dawn on me. Seeing Jesus soon might mean I was going to die! How soon? Now I was scared, too! I couldn't help it, tears started to roll down my cheeks. I didn't want to die yet. I didn't want to leave Mama. I was just a kid. How could dying soon be lucky or blessed?

Mama took a deep breath, and her face got more color back. "I know what this is," she said. "You've been preparing to make your First Holy Communion. Either you dreamed about meeting Jesus in this special way—" I started to protest that it couldn't have been a dream. She quickly added,

7

"Or maybe the Virgin Mary really did come to remind you how blessed you are to be receiving Him soon into your body and soul."

I searched my mother's eyes, looking for any sign that she was hiding something from me, but she seemed relieved and confident now. Yes, she must be right. This was all about meeting Jesus in the bread and wine of Communion. I would receive Jesus soon and see Him in the bread and wine with what Mama called my "faith eyes." Eyes that looked beyond what was visible to what was true.

Ten days later I knelt in one of the front pews of our little church with my classmates, waiting for the time to receive Jesus into my heart. The church smelled of incense, an aroma I still enjoy. I looked across the aisle at others and saw my friend Evan, who was aglow with a beam of sunlight from the stained-glass window. Evan was darker than I, so I had thought before about how Jesus, as a boy from the Middle East, might have looked like this friend. Now, with the light making his hair shine like a halo, I remembered Mary telling me I would see her Son soon. Was this what she meant? Evan was a nice kid, but he wasn't Jesus. At least I didn't think he was. Could Jesus be one of my classmates?

After the lector had read from the Old Testament and the choir had sung a responsorial song, I looked again at Evan, but the light beam had moved. Now it was illuminating the girl next to Evan, named Marcie. Marcie's red hair glowed like a halo, too, and in her white dress and veil she looked very angelic, but I knew differently. She was a bully, and I had learned to keep a good distance from her to avoid her teasing and mocking. No, the light beam definitely wasn't showing me who Jesus was, if that's what it was trying to do.

I pulled my attention back to the lector, who had finished the second reading, taken from the New Testament parts that weren't the Gospels. I felt bad for letting my mind wander. This was an important day. I'd be able to receive Communion from now on, taking Jesus into my heart and body. I'd have Jesus inside me. That gave me a new thought: everyone in my class, even Marcie, would as well. I wouldn't actually see Jesus when I looked at them, but Jesus would be there, inside each of them. Inside of me, too. My heart surged a beat at that thought. I wanted to keep Jesus inside me always. I wanted to remember that Jesus was inside everyone else, too. I'd need to remember to use my faith eyes to see Jesus in people.

The Gospel that day was one of my favorite stories, where Jesus says to let the children come to Him and tells grown-ups to be like children in order to enter His kingdom. I was fairly sure He didn't mean being childish, but maybe wanting to rush to Jesus like the children had—wanting to be near Him and feel His love and trust His care. I told myself I'd have to remember that when I became an adult. I'd try to always rush to Jesus and trust Him.

Finally, it was time for my class of white-dressed girls and suited boys to approach the altar and take our turns accepting the little wafer of bread that had become Jesus' body. We also received the blood of Christ with a little sip from the chalice. When it was my turn, I tasted bread and wine, but my faith eyes knew I had taken Jesus into my body. I returned to my place and quietly thanked Jesus for coming to me. I felt tears threatening and didn't wipe them away, not wanting people to notice I was crying, but they were happy tears. I loved Jesus, and now we could be together in such a special way every time I received Communion. Or Eucharist, as my teacher called it, telling us it meant giving thanks. So, I gave thanks, and I gave praise to Jesus in my heart. I felt quite grown up but very small at the same time. I asked Jesus to take care of Mama and Daddy and everyone I loved.

Had I seen Jesus, like Mary told me I would? I watched the rest of the church file up to receive Communion. I looked across the aisle when the procession to the altar had ended and saw Marcie smiling with her eyes closed. Jesus was inside her. Evan was grinning as he looked up at a statue. Jesus was inside him. Most of my class was smiling. I wondered why I hadn't seen any of the grownups smile. Didn't they realize what a gift they'd been given? Maybe it was hard to remember how special Communion was since they could do it every week, or even every day. That was another thing I told myself I'd have to remember when I grew up, to smile after Communion because God is inside me, and God loves me deeply. Jesus loves everyone enough to give them this chance to be one with Him in such a simple but deep way.

That was the day I began trying to see Jesus in everyone.

Frank closed his eyes, as if the effort of sharing this memory had worn him out. While he rested, Pedra transcribed what he had said from her shorthand notebook to her laptop. She thought this was just about the best task the Reverend Mother could have assigned her. Then she thought about what he had said. Could a person really grow to see Jesus in everyone they meet? She remembered the cranky patients who were so angry to be in the hospital. She thought of Mother Superior, who frightened her nearly every time she saw her. Pedra thought of her father. No, she could probably live her whole life and not see Jesus in everyone as easily as Frank made it sound.

Chapter 2

The next morning, Pedra looked forward to listening to Frank again. Morning prayer and community breakfast seemed to drag on, but finally she and the other sisters walked two-by-two to the hospital. As she entered Frank's room, she noticed the monitors humming peacefully, and that he didn't seem as tired as when she left the day before. He smiled as if she were his favorite person in the world.

"How are you feeling?" she asked.

"Can't complain," he said with a shrug.

"Why does your chart just say Frank?" Pedra asked, just one of many questions coming to mind.

He answered, "I think titles can get in the way of relationships. I want to be simply what my friends call me, which is Frank, in the hope that I can be a friend to each person that I meet. So, I'm Frank and you're, remind me?"

"Pedra."

"I'm Frank and you're Pedra, and we are peers and friends who can enjoy a simple chat. Welcome, Pedra. You look perplexed. Another question?"

"Could you really do it? Could you see Jesus in everyone? I can't imagine I could."

"I sure couldn't as a child. Skills need practice to be learned. Much like shorthand, I assume. But that gives me a good place to start for today's story."

She sat, opened her notebook to the next empty page, and he began.

I wasn't a particularly good student, or athlete, or musician. I was a day dreamer, as my teachers often wrote on my report cards. Some kids are hyper or easily distracted. I just enjoyed deep thinking. I always have been that way. My classmates teased me when they weren't bullying me. I upset the other boys, if I was on their team, because I never really cared enough about ball games to practice and get good at any. I failed any academic team when we competed in spelling bees or debates, or any contest really. I'd work and I'd manage passable grades, but never anything for my mother to brag about.

My dad really wanted to help me find my gifts. He tried to teach me chess but got frustrated when I'd ask why each piece moved the way it did. Why should a knight be able to only move three spaces in an L shape, when another piece could go as far as the player wanted in one direction? He offered to play catch with me, but I really just wanted to read, or better yet, think. Over the years, Dad enrolled me in so many classes: sports, art, music, drama, carpentry, and even auto mechanics, but I never developed an aptitude for any of them. He finally just gave up and figured I'd have to work it out on my own.

Pedra thought of her own father and wondered if he ever tried to encourage her to discover her talents. She certainly couldn't remember him doing so. In fact, he rarely gave her any attention at all, except to correct or chastise her. At times like that, her mother seemed to melt into the background, unwilling to defend Pedra or draw her husband's notice away from his daughter.

She returned her focus to Frank's words.

What I did like doing was reading the New Testament. Our Lady had told me I'd meet her Son, and I wanted to be ready. At first, I used a child's book of stories about Jesus, but eventually a simplified Bible, and before long a regular Bible. I liked the Jesus I met there. As a child, He must have been a deep thinker, and I could relate to that, and loved how He sat and listened to the elders at the temple and asked questions with understanding, even at twelve. He was kind and gentle with people, but could be passionate, like when money lenders misused his Father's temple. I was intrigued by his healing miracles, thinking that might be just about the coolest of gifts to be given, to be able to heal people of their brokenness and pain. As I learned about Him from reading, I was drawn to Him, and began talking to Him as a friend. I still do. I highly recommend it!

He looked at Pedra in silence until she glanced up and met his gaze. "I highly recommend it," he repeated. She underlined the words and considered her own prayers, always memorized or read. What would it be like to talk to God? *Not much of a two-sided conversation*, she thought. Then Frank continued his story.

Years passed and I never forgot the night that Mother Mary told me I would see Jesus soon. Sometimes, I felt disappointed that I hadn't "seen" Jesus in a way that I could have a conversation with Him. Sometimes I figured it was simply a dream. Yet, there weren't any other dreams from those younger years that I remembered. Dream or not, I knew that night had changed me. Since then, when people were unkind to me, even Mean Marcie, as the other kids still called her, I strove to see the good in them. Usually, I could find some attribute that reflected Jesus' goodness. Sometimes, I learned more about people's struggles, and that helped me better understand their behavior. I didn't approve of their bad choices, but I knew they were suffering in their own way, much like Jesus had suffered at the hands of the unkind. Marcie, for example, had a mother who made her daughter look kind by comparison. I once had seen her strike Marcie across the face.

He winced as he said this, then he continued.

They both needed prayers.
A few years later, my class of eighth graders, including Marcie and

me, were back in the church waiting for another sacrament, ready to be confirmed. Though some of my friends didn't seem to take it seriously, other than discussing how much money they might receive as gifts, being confirmed meant so much to me. I'd gladly chosen for myself that I'd be a Catholic for my whole life and as faithful a Catholic as I could be. I would attend Mass as often as I could but certainly every Sunday. I'd follow the precepts of the Church, obey the commandments, even Jesus' command that I "love others as I have loved you." I knew that could mean dying for others. I prayed I could have that kind of courage. But it also meant living for others, which required its own level of bravery. Above all, I strove to build a real relationship with Jesus by spending time with Him, whether in front of the Blessed Sacrament in adoration, or in conversation with Him in prayer, or through little love offerings by way of sacrifices.

Not long after our Confirmation and near the end of the school year, I entered the church hall along with about 100 teens from several parishes. This was an invitational youth group meeting, meant to welcome the other eighth graders and me, so that after our imminent graduation, we'd feel comfortable attending the teen group, a kind of graduation from the grade school religion classes that we'd be finishing. I looked around at my classmates. We were waiting as a group in the back, not sure what to do. We'd been together since kindergarten in our Catholic grade school. Soon we'd move on in different directions. Most of them would continue their education at Catholic high schools. Our city had three: one for girls, one for boys, and one co-ed, so our class would be divided among them. My folks had told me they couldn't afford the private tuition, so I'd attend the public high school, a few blocks away. I was pleased I'd still be able to gather with familiar peers weekly at the Youth Group. It would take a couple more years before I could work enough to pay Catholic high school tuition myself, since no one would hire me as an eighth grader. Personally, I was glad that I wasn't headed to an all-boys school. I didn't talk to the girls much, but I'd sure miss seeing them if they weren't around. Girls were just so... fascinating!

My thoughts were interrupted by one of the seniors in the group calling for our attention. He invited us to take seats and introduced us to the teen leaders who were also seniors like him. Then he introduced the new leaders, juniors who would take their place next year. A handful of adults supervised but allowed the teens to do most of the interacting. A boy and a girl, or maybe, I thought, I should call them a young man and a young woman, each gave a short talk about how the group had helped them deepen their faith or feel supported through challenging times.

Excitement made me grin. I'd been hoping for a place where I could talk among friends about our faith. I wanted to grow closer to Jesus, but not feel like I was weird for that desire.

That was when I first learned about the value of belonging to a community with shared beliefs.

Frank lay his head back against the pillow, smiling, perhaps reminiscing. Pedra finished her note taking and transcribed what had been said. As she did, she thought about her own situation. She was in formation, trying to become a permanent part of the community of sisters. Yet, she hadn't really thought about why belonging to a community of believers was important. She didn't share much of herself with either Jesus or the sisters, she realized, and hadn't tried to reach out to make friends. She made a mental note to work on that from now on. They had a common goal, after all, and could support one another as they grew closer to each other and Christ.

Chapter 3

On the third day, Frank grinned, showing a little gap in his smile, when Pedra entered his room. She realized that he had been looking forward to her arrival. The idea warmed her, and affection for the bedridden man bloomed.

When Pedra sat down next to Frank, he said, "You know, Pedra, this has been a fairly one-sided discussion. I'd like to get to know you better. Can you tell me a little about yourself?"

"But this is supposed to be all about you. That's why I'm here, to get your story down on paper. Not mine."

"Humor me," he urged. "It's easier to talk when you know your audience. How about if I get to ask you one question per day?"

"How about one occasional question?" she countered. Actually, it had been a long time since anyone had shown much interest in her life. Pedra wasn't used to talking about herself. Even the interview to be considered for the convent had been difficult, but she must have been acceptable, at least for a trial period. Yes, one question, now and then, she could probably handle.

"Fair enough. Here's today's," Frank said. "What was your childhood like?"

Pedra set her pencil down on her tablet. How to answer? She didn't want to share about unhappy times, but to be honest, she didn't have many other kinds of times. Yet Frank had been so open with her, she felt she could trust him not to judge.

"My dad was strict. My mom was... distant. They weren't

the warm, affectionate types."

He didn't respond but seemed to be waiting for more.

"I didn't have siblings, so I spent a lot of time alone. I guess I got used to it."

He nodded.

She wondered why she was withholding more about herself. She trusted him. After a long exhale, she continued, "Actually, my parents were both deaf. They communicated with sign language. I didn't hear speech as an infant or toddler. When a pediatrician realized I was way behind in speech, they started me in a preschool, and I learned to talk there. But I always wondered if it was too late. Maybe I missed out on some important skills during those silent years."

"You must be very good at sign language."

She smiled at how he could always focus on the positive. "I guess I am. And maybe it helped me learn shorthand, to understand how visual symbols could stand in for spoken words."

"I'm sure God has a plan for how to use all your life experiences."

Pedra shrugged and Frank kindly took the focus from her.

"I know which story I want to tell you next," he said with excitement.

Pedra answered, "Well then let's begin!" She scooted her chair toward his bed, happy to face him and watch the animation of his expression.

"I better start at the beginning. I loved Youth Group," he said before she'd gotten ready to take shorthand. "We mostly focused on service."

Pedra quickly opened her pad and caught up to him as best she could. He seemed excited about this part of his story and spoke quickly.

At first it felt awkward, going to help people. I thought they might be embarrassed by the contrast between their need and our privileged lives, but most of them were truly grateful. We sorted clothes at a local St. Vincent de Paul and were encouraged to converse with those who shopped there. We ran food drives in our neighborhoods. Later we distributed those cans and packages to shelves at the local food bank or boxed up supplies to deliver to families. We helped manage the lines of people indoors, or the cars outdoors, as people drove up trying to stretch their food budget to reach the end of the month.

Other times we visited nursing homes for the elderly, and we'd sing some old-time songs or simply spread out and visit with the residents. I learned to admire the kind employees who worked in the homes every day, whether cleaning up after accidents, helping with showers, or being cheerful and patient even when the residents weren't. Some folks there felt forgotten and abandoned, and their hurt could turn to anger. Once, though, I saw one of the crankiest old men turn into a baby-talking cuddler when a therapy dog nudged his hand for a pet. I think we all need a little nudge out of our self-pity occasionally.

In December we would arrange and throw a Christmas party for foster kids. We'd each pick a toy for someone whose name we'd drawn, but we'd also have raised money so that each child was able to take home a suitcase or duffle bag for the meager possessions that travelled with them from home to home. Seeing those kids and hearing some of their stories sure made me grateful for my mom and dad. We didn't have a lot of money, so not many things, but we did have lots of love. I grew up with a sense of security that those kids might not ever have known. I still pray for foster kids and that genuinely good people will be inspired to become foster parents.

We had some exceptional adults who helped with the Youth Group. Some of them were college kids who wanted to give back a bit of what they gained in their high school years. Others were married couples whose teens had graduated and moved on, but they still enjoyed sharing their faith with us. I always found it interesting to watch those married couples interact. They made me long to be part of a healthy, faith-filled couple. As a freshman and sophomore, sometimes I'd look around at the girls in our group, wondering if any of them might be my special someone. I was too shy *at that time to act on that idea.*

In my junior year of high school, though, I fell in love, convinced I'd found the treasure of my life.

Pedra glanced at Frank's left hand—no wedding ring, nor mark where one had been worn for years. This love story must have ended badly, she reasoned. She hadn't seen anyone visiting the elderly man and that surprised her, now that she knew how pleasant he was.

He sighed, perhaps confirming her thought that the story had a sad ending, and then he continued.

You aren't going to guess who I fell in love with. She was in the Youth Group and, not surprisingly, we were often paired off for projects. Not surprising, I say, because she was still called Mean Marcie, and she and I were the only two left when people chose their work partners. At first, I even considered quitting Youth Group, but I felt bad at the thought that she'd be all alone. I decided to secretly make her my own service project. I'd be as kind as I could, no matter what she said to me. I'd offer it up as a sacrifice. It was rough for a while as we got used to each other, but then something happened. I started seeing the good in her. She had a wicked sense of humor. I'd been on the wrong end of that enough times to have already learned about her wit. However, she also had a very tender heart for the outcast. In fact, now that I think about it, maybe I was her project. I certainly was a loner, and not by choice.

As we earned service hours, I realized that Marcie wasn't going to do the minimum. In fact, whether we were bringing sandwiches to the homeless, or playing with developmentally delayed children, she always made a beeline to the worst cases. Strung out drug addicts didn't scare her. Kids who only had the abilities of helpless infants didn't deter her. Here I was still trying to see Jesus in everyone while not contracting lice, and she simply assumed the "poorest of the poor" were her people. My admiration for her grew every time we worked together. She must have decided to put up with me, because it seemed like we moved from being adversaries, to tolerating each other, to working well together.

Then one day, we were sorting cans from a food drive, and she leaned over and kissed me. It was just a quick peck, but it was on my lips, and I could have floated right to heaven. Well, I might have if she hadn't slugged me in the shoulder in the next moment. I drove her home after our meeting that night, and every night after that when I could. We went to dances together. We kissed more often and for longer, but only when it was her idea. I learned that if I leaned in for a kiss, or even just tried to hold her hand, she was likely to walk away. That was okay with me. I was already struggling with teenage hormones and figured it was probably just as well that she enforced limits. As much as I wanted to obey the Church's wise counsel about premarital sex, my body was often reacting well before my head caught up.

I grew to love my Marcie so much. I could see Jesus in our relationship. Like Him, I wanted to provide her with everything good. I wanted to encourage her to be her best; while assuring her I loved her just the way she was. And someday, I hoped our affection for each other would create children to share our love.

I would have done anything to protect her if I could. That's when I learned about the pain of loving someone.

Frank's voice choked with those words, and his heart monitor began to alarm. A crash team flew into the room and chased Pedra out. She stood in the hall listening, hoping, and praying. That's when *she* learned about the pain of loving someone.

∞

Pedra looked at her watch and realized she needed to leave to be in time for prayers at the convent. That evening, after the other sisters had left the chapel, Pedra settled onto the kneeler in her pew for her turn at Adoration, keeping Jesus company. She thought about Frank's suggestion that she talk to Jesus as a friend. She'd prayed many times a day since entering the novitiate, but always using memorized prayers. Could she talk to Jesus the way Frank did? She decided to try.

Hi, Jesus, it's me, Pedra.

Now what? Since Jesus is God and knows everything, she wondered what to say that He didn't already know.

Hi, Jesus, she started again. *You know where I've been, who I've been talking to, and what I've been doing. I guess I could share my thoughts with You. I assume You know those, too, but Frank says I should, and Jesus, I really trust him. So, here goes.*

Please take care of Frank. In just these few days I've come to treasure my time with him. I don't know why he is so alone, or much about his health, though I've been told he's at risk. I don't know if this is okay to ask, but could you please heal him? I know he's old, but maybe give him a few more years. I could learn so much from him.

She felt a little embarrassed, not knowing quite what to say, but she trusted Frank that she could talk to Jesus like a friend, so she continued.

I'm a little worried about my future. I think Mother Superior is going to send me away, saying this convent isn't a very good fit for me. All the professed sisters are nurses. I know I don't quite blend in. I guess I've never quite fit anywhere. I haven't learned how to manage small talk, or have real conversations, for that matter. Maybe that's why it's hard even to talk to You.

I don't know what I want. Will I be disappointed if they send me away? I like the quiet here, but I suspect I'm hiding from the life I'm supposed to be leading. What do You want me to do? I guess I should have asked that long ago, before I entered the convent. Before I quit my job. I'm lonely. I thought living with other women would help that, but I can't say I've made friends here. Maybe my only friend is Frank, and he might be dying, for all I know. Is he dying, Jesus? He seems too, well, wise, to die. But I know his heart caused trouble yesterday.

What will I do if he dies? In so few days I've come to really love that man. Not husband/wife kind of love, but admiration and awe. I would miss him so very much. I've loved taking down the story of his life. I guess I love the feeling I get when he appreciates me spending time and writing for him. I came here hoping to help people. I think I'm really helping him.

Pedra didn't see Jesus. And she didn't hear His voice, even a "still, small voice" in her mind, but she did feel better. She could see why Frank encouraged her to talk to Jesus like a friend. She could certainly use a friend. She feared her only friend in the world wouldn't be in this world much longer.

Chapter 4

Noticeably weaker the next day when Pedra visited, Frank still grinned and waved her in.

"Are you okay?" she asked.

"Just a little heart episode yesterday."

"Is that why you're in the rehab center? Your heart?"

"I'm here because I had a stroke, but my heart is acting up, too. Still, I can't complain."

"Why not? I think I'd complain." Actually, she *knew* she'd complain if she were bedbound and without visitors in a hospital.

"I'm blessed. I have so much to be grateful for," he said.

Pedra knew she should count her blessings, too, but she'd never felt loved. She'd never had someone special like Frank had Marcie. She'd given up and joined a convent, for heaven's sake; she lived surrounded by women, yet still felt alone.

"You seem sad," Frank said.

She shrugged. "Can't complain." She'd copied his words and realized she felt a bit better just for saying it. "Are we going to continue where we left off? With Marcie?" She watched his smile falter and wished she hadn't mentioned Marcie. She must be a painful subject for Frank.

"Let me tell you a happier story," he said, and this time he waited for her to have her pencil ready before he began.

By our Junior year, I was making enough money with odd jobs that

I was able to pay tuition for the Catholic high school. One priest I particularly liked was Fr. Ray Joyce. Sometimes we called him Father Rejoice. Or just Father Joy. He taught religion and also attended our Youth Group, so I got to know him pretty well. He seemed happy most of the time, with a smile both huge and contagious. He told great tales about his own growing up, but also stories about people he knew and admired. He made me want to become someone he admired. I intensified my commitment to the Youth Group and soon became one of the leaders. I had a knack for organization, even if I was still weak in people skills. He'd tell me about a new idea for service, and I'd research it, make the necessary plans, and we'd make it happen.

Once, we organized a dance for homeschool teens. Encouraged by that success, we hosted another dance for teens with disabilities. We raised money to sponsor turkeys for the food bank near Thanksgiving and Christmas. We painted the outside of the church, and the inside of a few elderly people's homes. You know, I don't remember much at all about my classes that year, but I certainly remember our service projects.

Frequently, I asked Fr. Joy about a priest's life. How could he give up having his own children and a wife? Did priests get lonely among their parish families? Was celibacy hard? He assured me that yes, the sacrifices were real and difficult, but the blessings of priesthood made it a wonderful choice. He encouraged me to consider it, and I did.

That fall and winter of my junior year, I felt like life couldn't get any better. I had a girlfriend and could imagine a happy, married life with children. Yet, I also had an alternative, becoming a priest, which spoke to my soul and could put my strengths to use for others. I'd talk to Marcie about considering being a priest, and she would tell me of her dreams to work for the Peace Corps, or the Red Cross, or Jesuit Volunteers and travel the world. I wasn't ready to decide about my future, but either way seemed like the road ahead shone brightly. I felt incredibly blessed.

Of course, our lives have their ups and downs, and I was headed for a series of devastations. I'll tell you more about that, but I think this is a good place to stop and remember the better times.

He switched gears and studied Pedra. "I've told you a little about weighing my vocational decisions. Your turn," Frank said. "Why did you enter the convent? Did you feel a call from God?"

Pedra was embarrassed to admit her reason, especially knowing how important a relationship with God was to this man. She took a deep breath, determined to be honest. "No, I can't say I felt called. Not long ago, but before the vaccines, I brought Covid home to my parents before I knew I was infected. I recovered quickly, but my mother did not. She contracted pneumonia and died. My father took it hard, of course, and he couldn't forgive me. When he had recovered, he sold his house and moved into a senior facility for the hearing impaired. I've tried to visit him there, but he refused to see me. After that, we were estranged. A few months later he caught Covid again and passed away."

"Don't give up on him, Pedra. I firmly believe that our loved ones can help us even more after they've passed and have been healed of their emotional wounds. I'm betting he's watching out for you with love," Frank said.

She would have to think about that, she decided, and continued with her story. "I was supporting myself in a little studio apartment by taking shorthand for lawyers' depositions and such, but I was lonely. I suspected I wasn't likely to find love after 30, having had no experience dating throughout my 20s. So, it seemed like a logical step. Join a convent and try to do some good for someone."

"Wanting to serve the world is a noble reason," Frank said.

"Unless…," Pedra replied.

He waited.

"Unless I'm fooling myself and really just wanted to not live alone for the rest of my life. Maybe I was running away from the world instead of drawing closer to God."

"You are certainly doing a service for me. I've enjoyed meeting you, and I feel comfortable telling you my story. You're a gifted listener."

"That's kind of you to say. I'm certainly not a gifted

conversationalist. I know that. When I get back to the convent after work each day, I go to prayer times, I attend Mass, but I don't talk to the other sisters. At first, they tried to ask questions and include me in their chatting, but eventually they gave up. I never know what to say. I never learned how to do small talk."

"It isn't hard, really," Frank offered. "You just have to find the right questions to ask. You need to show that you've been listening and take an interest in what they say. How was their day? Are they reading any good books? What's new with their families, or their patients, or their students? And here's a secret my mother taught me: look into their eyes and smile. It works wonders to help people be comfortable around you."

She couldn't help herself, she looked into his kind eyes and grinned.

"Yes, just like that!" He laughed. "You have a very pretty smile. It lights up your eyes."

The compliment embarrassed her, and she looked down.

"I found it takes practice," he said softly. "Start with smiling at yourself in the mirror. That alone will give your mood a lift, if you're anything like me."

∞

Pedra returned to the convent after work, remembering Frank's words. As she entered the common room, she forced herself to smile. A few of the sisters were chatting in easy chairs, and two were working on a puzzle together at a table. When Sister Agatha glanced her way, Pedra said, "Hello. How was your day, Sister Agatha?"

To her surprise, Sister Agatha beamed at her. "I had a letter from my brother. It made my day. Thank you for asking!"

Normally, Pedra would have nodded and moved on, but spurred by Frank's encouragement, she said, "Good news, I hope?"

"Yes, his wife is expecting! They've been wanting a child for a long time, so this is wonderful to hear. I wish I could be there to give them both a hug."

Pedra's heart was racing, and she could feel her cheeks burn, but she told herself it was excitement, not anxiety. "Do they live far away?"

"Oh yes," Agatha said, "they live in England, where I grew up."

"I didn't realize that," said Pedra. "It must be so different for you here. What do you miss from England? And how did you end up at this convent?"

Evidently, Pedra had found the perfect questions, and Agatha chatted on for several minutes. Other sisters joined in, and Pedra felt a warm glow of fondness for these ladies. Why had she not engaged with them before this? She silently thanked Frank for his suggestions.

Three other postulants lived at the convent and would hold more of a challenge for Pedra to befriend, she guessed. They were younger than she and seemed to belong to a different culture all together. At recreation time that evening, they talked of music groups and sang songs she'd never heard. One played the guitar, and Pedra asked her how she learned to play. The girl reminisced about her father teaching her, and her story gave Pedra a lovely image in her mind of a family gathered close and sharing their enjoyment of music. Pedra wondered what her parents had shared with her, or even what they had loved. Music wasn't a part of their lives, of course. They were both readers; she remembered the long, silent nights. There was no television or radio in their home, even when closed captions became available. She'd grown to be a reader, too, out of desperation, and the library served as her home away from home. Another silent world.

Pedra brought herself back to the present and reminded herself to appreciate sharing music with… friends? Were they friends? She had interacted so little with them, but looking at them now, three happy, smiling young women, she realized they could grow close. Then she looked around the room at the older sisters. Some were tapping their feet to the postulants' music. Others were chatting quietly while they knitted or crocheted. A couple were reading. Pedra couldn't help but smile. She met eyes with Mother Superior, who looked deep in thought. Then even Mother Superior smiled and nodded.

∞

Bernard Lovejoy had come to the end of what research he could do online to find his half-brother. He would turn in grades for his classes in a week, the beginning of his summer break, and then he would travel across the state to Daniel Roma's birth city. He'd reserved a short-term rental and hoped that two weeks would be enough to locate, contact, and meet this stranger whom he felt optimistic would be open to connecting. His research had narrowed down all the Daniel Romas to this one. He was the only one with a birth recorded in the right year. On the birth certificate, his mother was listed as Marcie Roma, father unknown.

He'd researched a few other Daniel Roma's but hit dead ends. They weren't born the exact year the genetics company had said, or they had died young. One person had looked promising, until he realized he was she, and her name was Roma Daniels.

The Daniel across the state, however, had been mentioned in an announcement of graduating seniors in the right year from a local high school. The next "hit" the internet had provided Bernard was an article twelve years later stating Daniel Roma, son of Frank, had been ordained a priest along with ten others. So, he was on the trail of Reverend Daniel Roma with a father, no longer "unknown," named Frank. Frank Roma, he assumed, though it was odd that the article didn't say that, and also that he found no mention of a Frank Roma in census reports or news articles. He'd scoured the diocese website and found no mention of Fr. Daniel Roma in lists of clergy assignments.

After he was settled into his rental, his next step would be to request a meeting with the bishop.

Chapter 5

The next morning at breakfast, Pedra asked Sister Margaret Mary, who was sitting across the table from her, where she grew up. Before long she had learned that the older woman was raised on a farm and still missed the animals, especially the dogs. The nuns seated on each side of them told stories about the dogs they owned as children, and Pedra felt another connection form.

When Pedra arrived at his hospital room, Frank seemed stronger and ready to continue his story. However, as Pedra settled into Frank's bedside chair, ready to take notes, an announcement came over the intercom in the hallway. "If anyone knows American Sign Language, please come to the ER, stat!"

She raised her eyebrows and asked Frank, "Did you tell them?"

"Not a word. You should go, though."

She sighed but stood. "I'll be back."

"I'll be waiting to hear all about it. At least, what can be shared. Privacy issues, you know."

She hurried to the emergency waiting room, half expecting, half hoping to see someone else there who had answered the call. She introduced herself to the receptionist and offered her help.

"Oh, thank God," the young woman said. "Come in!" She buzzed the door open, and Pedra entered.

Several people in white coats or blue scrubs surrounded a woman who was obviously in great pain and very frightened, thrashing on the bed. Pedra pushed through, got the woman's attention with a touch and signed, "What's wrong? What do you need them to know?"

"We tried to write questions for her to write answers, but she's too distraught," a nurse explained.

The woman frantically signed that her stomach felt like a sword had been thrust into it. Pedra became her voice and repeated her words to the staff. A doctor asked Pedra to sign his questions to the woman and explain what he was doing as he palpitated her abdomen. Before long they had concluded she probably had an acute gall bladder attack and would need surgery. She was able to tell Pedra that she was pregnant and begged the staff to keep her baby safe. They nodded their assurances to the woman when Pedra told them, and they had Pedra ask for permission to do surgery. By now, pain medication had begun to take effect. The woman calmed considerably, and she signed her agreement. She then squeezed Pedra's hand before signing, "Thank you."

They asked Pedra to come with them, as they wheeled the woman to the operating room, and stay until she was under the effects of anesthesia. Before she was asleep, Pedra learned from her whom they should contact. The doctor also asked Pedra to return when she moved to recovery, so they could communicate if next of kin hadn't arrived.

As Pedra returned to Frank's floor, word came to that nurse's station that the woman's husband was on his way, and he would interpret for his wife and the staff. Pedra sank into Frank's chair, greatly relieved. After telling Frank about the experience and getting out her steno pad, Pedra ventured to ask, "Frank, what happened to Marcie?"

∞

The old man frowned, and she again worried the question would be too much for him.

Ah, Marcie. Yes, Marcie is an essential part of my story. I had grown to love her and, as we approached Easter of our junior year, I bought her a promise ring. I couldn't afford a diamond yet, and I figured we couldn't get married for a few years, but I wanted her to know she was the one for me.

We had a date for the Prom, and I figured I'd give the ring to her then. I had saved to take her out to dinner beforehand. Nothing fancy, but a place with tablecloths. I arrived and rang the doorbell of their run-down home, hoping her mother wouldn't answer. She was never really mean to me, but I could tell she wasn't thrilled that Marcie and I were dating.

However, her mother did answer and frowned to see me standing there in my suit and holding a corsage.

"Marcie isn't here," she said, and started to close the door.

"Will she be home soon?" I asked. "I could wait or come back. Where is she?"

"If she wanted you to know, she would have called you," came the answer. "She's gone. I doubt she'll be back."

"I don't understand. What happened?" I insisted.

Her mother crossed her arms and looked smug. "Police came and took her away."

"What!?!" I couldn't believe it.

"They came with a search warrant and found her drug stash," her mother said, and almost sounded jubilant.

"Marcie doesn't do drugs."

"Well, she must sell them then." And she closed the door.

I went to the police station, but they wouldn't let me see Marcie. However, a couple days later, Marcie did call. It turned out there were no fingerprints of Marcie's on the bags, but her mother's prints were all over them. They were going to release Marcie but into her father's custody, because they had arrested her mother and her mother's boyfriend. As far as I knew, she hadn't seen her father in years, but he lived hundreds of miles away, and the thought of Marcie being so far crushed me.

"Can I at least see you first?" I begged.

She said, "Daddy doesn't want me to, as he put it, 'associate with anyone local.' I guess he isn't convinced the drugs weren't mine. He won't even give me his address so you could write."

I loved her, yet she was slipping through my fingers and there was nothing I could do.

"You could write to me once you're there. Or maybe you could convince him to let you live with us, at least until you finish your senior year!"

"I have to go," she said. "He's here."

And that was the last time I heard from her for months. Then I received a letter. It's folded up in my wallet. I've never been able to part with it, and it has accompanied me wherever I go.

Pedra opened the drawer he pointed to and found an old, frayed wallet, which held less than $20, a few photos, and a yellowed, creased, and tattered paper. She opened it and read:

Dear Frank,

I've missed you so much. I think you might be the only person in the world who really loves me. I'm in trouble. I knew when I left, but I didn't want to tell you.

Frank, I'm pregnant. Very pregnant. I can't do this alone. I need you. If I come back, will you marry me right away, so the baby has a father who can love it? But please promise me you won't ask who the real father is. I can't talk about it.

Just know, it's you I love… at least as much as I'm able to love someone.

Marcie

After her signature was a phone number.

"You called her! What happened?" Pedra asked. She didn't know why, but she had assumed he was a priest. But maybe not. Maybe he had married Marcie.

After a nod and a deep sigh, Frank continued his story.

I called her right away and told her yes, I'd marry her. I had just turned 18, so wouldn't need my parents' permission, though I knew they'd be against it. But I loved her, and she needed me. I couldn't leave her alone to handle this. I knew it would be hard not to ask her about the father. I mostly wanted to know if she chose him, or if he forced her. She always pulled back if I tried more than kissing, so I assumed the latter.

Marcie arrived the next day and she was right, she was very pregnant. We got a license, I skipped school for the first time ever, and we got married at the courthouse with the little promise ring I'd bought months earlier. Then we told my parents. Mom cried. Dad went for a walk. I suppose they assumed the baby was mine, and I never told them differently. I never told anyone. It was my gift to Marcie. Luckily, my mom and dad let us stay with them, upstairs in my old room. They wanted me to finish high school and I did. Marcie took the GED test and got an equivalency diploma.

I remember the rush of emotions the first time I took my son into my arms. He was so tiny, so perfect. I wanted to protect him from all harm and difficulty. I wanted to always be able to surround him in an embrace and hold him close. What a miracle a child is!

Mom and Dad were great when the baby came. They loved him instantly and immediately were devoted grandparents. At the hospital, I learned all I could about baby care, right alongside Marcie. I never knew I could love anyone so deeply and completely. It didn't matter that I hadn't been there at his conception. I was there at his birth, and he was ours.

When we brought him home from the hospital, Mom and Dad had gotten the old crib and highchair out of the attic. They had saved a few of my baby clothes, but we bought more used and settled into his care as a team. Marcie named him Daniel Frank Roma, the Frank for me but Daniel Roma after her dad. I couldn't understand why she didn't want Daniel to have my last name. Maybe she just needed something of herself to give him. Maybe she and her dad had grown close while she lived with him. He came for the baptism and seemed like a nice enough guy, though I could tell I wasn't his favorite person in the world. Her mother didn't come. I don't know if she was still in jail or not, but I was relieved anyway. I think Marcie was, too.

Of course, parenting isn't easy. We struggled through the frequent feedings, the lack of sleep, the financial worries, and keeping us all healthy. In the early days, the care of an infant seemed a thankless job, but I didn't mind. Eventually, when he learned to smile, that felt reward enough.

Things went pretty well for a few months. Marcie and I explored being married, even physically, but I won't go into that, other than to say each time we made love, it felt like she'd given me a wonderful gift. I started working full time after graduation to support my little family. I had really hoped to go to college, but it just wasn't feasible with my new responsibilities. I didn't want us to be a financial burden to my folks. Mom helped Marcie and me learn about taking care of a baby, and she stepped in when she knew Marcie was exhausted. Daniel needed feeding about every two hours at first, and I knew it was too much for Marcie. She didn't want to nurse, so we took turns with bottle feeding. Before long I was an old hand at diapering, feeding, burping, and rocking to sleep.

One Saturday, I noticed Marcie watching me feed Daniel, her head tilted and her expression very sober. I smiled, and she nodded but wouldn't share what she was thinking.

The next Monday when I came home from work, my mother looked stricken as she met me at the door with Daniel in her arms. Marcie Roma had left me again, but this time she had left Daniel as well.

Pedra stopped writing and looked up at Frank, feeling the pain he must have known so long ago and seeing its remnant in his eyes.

"I found a short note," Frank said. "I didn't save it, but its words are burned into my heart. 'Thanks for loving Daniel and me. The world needs me more than you two do. I know he'll be fine in your care.'"

"I'm so sorry," was all Pedra could say.

Frank appeared lost in the memory, so Pedra took her leave.

∞

That evening in chapel, she talked again to Jesus.

I'm not sure what direction You want me to take, Jesus. I'm enjoying listening and transcribing for Frank. That makes me feel alive and like I'm contributing something with my life.

And the dear lady in the emergency room, I helped her, too. She was so scared to not be able to communicate. It made me feel good to be there for her. I wouldn't have been able to help if my parents hadn't been deaf and taught me sign language. I guess I should be grateful that they did. I've spent so much time blaming them for my communication problems. But looking back, maybe my parents did the best they could. They fed me and kept me safe. I just wish they had shown me that they loved me. I don't remember any cuddles or hugs. No lap time. No, "How was your day?" I felt they weren't very interested in me. That's probably where I first got the sense that I wasn't very appealing. Or worth anyone's time.

But Frank seems to think I am. He asks me questions and listens to what I have to say about myself. I think You are listening, too, and that gives me the same warm feeling that Frank's attention does.

Chapter 6

When Pedra had settled into her chair the next day, she had to ask, "Did Marcie ever come back?"

He shook his head no. "And I'm afraid it's another sad story I have to tell you, but you should know that it eventually leads to happiness."

Frank began:

I was angry—really, really angry. I couldn't believe Marcie had left us. I felt like she had used me, just to have someone to leave Daniel with, so then she could be free of responsibility. I have to admit I was angry with God, too. Why did He let this happen? Why did He let me love her so deeply and then lose her? I had been torn between being a family man and being a priest, and it seemed Marcie stole the decision from me. Plus, I was exhausted. I tried to do all that our son needed, but with my sleep interrupted for feedings, my worry about finances, and the sheer emotional devastation, I was a mess. Looking back now, I thank God that my parents were there to help me those first few months.

I never resented Daniel. That sweet little boy was the bright spot in a dark time. However, each time he cried, I thought of Marcie and grew angrier that she wasn't there to help us. Holding him though, watching him stare into my eyes as he drank a bottle, and eventually his smiles helped to heal the wound in my soul. I realized I couldn't hold on to my anger and be a good father to him. He'd feel the tension in my arms and cry more easily or see my scowl and frown in response. When I realized my hurt ran too deep to easily forgive Marcie, I began to pray, both for help to forgive, and for her wellbeing. I think that helped. It took months, after she left, before I could think about her without seething. But as I watched Daniel try to toddle on his own, I imagined my "forgiveness muscles" also toddling and growing stronger.

Frank paused until Pedra looked up from her tablet. He sighed and she waited.

Just when I thought I was gaining my equilibrium, My mom and dad were killed in a car accident. I could have slipped back into despair and anger with God, but He gave me the grace I needed. I imagine if I hadn't done the work to forgive Marcie, my heart would have been hardened and this next loss would have turned it into stone. With God's help, I managed to keep going. I also learned about the necessity of forgiveness if we want to see Jesus in people. Or in ourselves, for that matter.

Parenting is a training ground for learning to sacrifice. Being a father taught me to put the needs of another person first. I learned to love sacrificially like Jesus teaches us when He asks us to perform works of mercy, like feeding the hungry (every two hours?), clothing the naked, and visiting the sick. Or spiritually as we instruct, comfort, counsel, admonish, or forgive.

As he grew, I battled constant fear of mistakes and feelings of inadequacy, not to mention loneliness. But Daniel was a gift. At first, he taught me to see Jesus, even in a tantruming two-year-old. He let me understand, to a small degree, what God the Father feels for each of us, even when we throw adult tantrums. Worries about Daniel spurred me to pray constantly.

Some insurance money was left over after the burials of my parents, so between that and working for another year after high school, my savings allowed me to start my freshman year of college in our hometown. The previous year off was good for me. I needed to grieve. I needed to learn to be self-sufficient. That was easy compared to learning how to parent alone. But the college offered a daycare, and I met other parents and made some good friends. I missed my folks, but I couldn't wallow. Daniel needed me to focus on him.

The college was run by priests, and I befriended several. I joined service groups, much like the Youth Group in high school. I met other people who valued their faith as highly as I did. I met some nice girls, but I wasn't free to date since I was still married, and they'd move on. I liked most of my classes, but especially theology, philosophy, and psychology. I surprised myself by actually excelling in those areas. They appealed to my deep-thinking nature. Having my parents' house was a financial blessing. I didn't need to pay for lodging, and Daniel and I didn't spend much. Plus, I didn't want to move so that if Marcie came back, or at least wrote, she would know where we were.

After that first year, I tried to decide whether to work for the summer to rebuild my funds or take summer school classes. I did both. One of my professors found me a part-time job at a homeless shelter that offered childcare. I did some cleaning and cooking, but mostly I did what you are doing for me. I listened to stories and offered friendship to the friendless. And I learned another side of life. Like Mary and Joseph who fled to Egypt with their newborn Son, some of the homeless were immigrants. Some were down on their luck and had lost their homes. Some were addicted to drugs or alcohol or both. They were nailed to their own kind of cross, seemingly without escape. But they all needed to be listened to, to be treated with dignity, to be fed and clothed and sheltered. Those people taught me so much. I learned how little in life is really necessary. How relationship is everything. I learned how Jesus was able to hug the lepers. These folks were just as much outcasts as lepers once were, so I figured they were His people. It wasn't always easy, but I occasionally succeeded at seeing Jesus in them.

One man came in every day for the noon meal. He always wore a tee shirt and jeans, much like most of the men there, but he looked more clean-cut than others. It took me a couple of weeks to notice that he moved around the diners chatting here and there, and occasionally took one or another of them into a separate room. I asked my supervisor about it, and he said, "Oh, you must mean Doc. He comes to bandage a blister, offer an antibiotic when something is infected, or encourage somebody to go to the *free health clinic for more care. I even saw him stitch up a knife wound once."*

I asked if he really was a doctor. My boss shrugged his shoulders. "Who knows," he said. "But he knows his stuff. He never asks for anything more than his lunch, and the people trust him. He's one of the good guys."

Those words made me want someone to say that about me someday. "He's one of the good guys."

Pedra glanced up from her steno pad. She saw Frank's eyes drift closed and could tell he needed a rest, so she quietly began to transcribe his story. When she came to his words, "Mostly I did what you are doing for me. I listened to stories and offered friendship to the friendless," she stopped. Was that what he thought of their time together? She was offering him friendship? The idea warmed her, and she felt proud of herself, a feeling she hadn't enjoyed in a very long time.

∞

That night during prayer time, Pedra asked, *Jesus, please guide my future. Show me where I should go and what I should do. Please don't make it too scary, though. I'm not like Frank's Marcie, who wanted to go where people were in the most need. Please don't call me to another country, or even far from home. But if You do, then I ask You to give me the courage to be obedient. I want to please You. I want You to see me at the gates of heaven someday and say, "She was one of the good guys."*

Chapter 7

The next day many questions were swirling in Pedra's head, but she sensed the memories Frank was sharing with her were painful, so she decided to let him lead the story to wherever he wanted to take her.

"Where were we?" he asked.

"You've finished your freshman year at college and worked the summer in a homeless shelter."

Ah, yes. Daniel was walking by then. I took him nearly everywhere with me, except class, of course. At first, he rode in a front pack, then as he grew more interested in his surroundings, I carried him in a backpack. I chose work that allowed him to be with me, like delivering groceries, or driving people across campus. I had a playpen he could be in while I gardened for folks, and for a while I worked at a daycare where we could be together. We constantly juggled and struggled, but by the time he entered full-day kindergarten, I graduated from college.

We were happy together. Daniel especially. He had one of those cheerful personalities, which certainly didn't come from Marcie or me. A gift from God, I guess. He seemed up for whatever adventures life had in store for us.

He did ask about his mother, of course. I had little I could tell him. Occasionally we would receive a postcard with a postmark from another country but no address, saying that she was happy and making a difference. I might have answered her the same if I ever knew where to send a letter. We were happy, and at least in one little life, I was making a difference. I told Daniel that his mother loved him so much that she left him with me, knowing I'd love him enough for both of us.

Her final postcard came from Africa. A pandemic had just begun to surge there, so of course, that's where she'd be. I remembered being frightened of contracting lice from homeless people. She, on the other hand, had no fear of the risk of dying from what we now know was AIDs.

Frank stopped to pull out a large handkerchief. He blew his nose before looking at Pedra with tear-filled eyes. "But that's what happened."

He continued.

One day when I'd picked up Daniel from school, and we'd returned to our little house, a woman was on our porch knocking on the door.

She turned when we approached. "Frank and Daniel?" she asked.

I nodded but my stomach dropped with a sense of foreboding.

"I'm from the Red Cross. I'm afraid I have sad news." She looked at Daniel, perhaps wondering if she should speak in front of him.

I squatted to fold my arms around him and pulled his back against my chest. We waited.

"Your wife, Marcie Roma, has passed away in Africa from AIDS as a result of the great sacrifices she made to work with the most destitute of people. Though it might be little comfort, you should be very proud of her dedication." She handed me an envelope that included a death certificate and the tiny promise ring. Perhaps she said more, but my mind wasn't taking much in after the words, "Your wife has passed away."

I thanked her, and when she had left, I sank down onto our porch step. I wept, clinging to our son for comfort, instead of comforting him. He patted me on the back, the way I'd done for him countless times when he'd been hurt or sad.

I looked into his eyes but saw only concern, not pain. I asked if he was okay. He shrugged. He'd never known her. He didn't remember ever seeing her. That broke my heart even more. Her loss wouldn't leave a hole *in his life, the way it did mine. I had never let go of the hope that she'd return, ready to be ours again.*

Frank's heart monitor began to chime, a reminder to relax and calm himself. He took a deep breath and smiled at Pedra, as if to reassure her that he was going to be fine.

Chapter 8

Frank was sitting up in a recliner when Pedra entered his room the next day. An aide was changing his sheets, and she called an orderly to help her get Frank back to bed. It was the first time Pedra realized the extent of Frank's stroke damage. He couldn't move his right arm or leg. She'd had no idea. Up until now, he'd been lying under the bedcovers. She must not have noticed that when he gestured, it was always with his left hand.

Not wanting to stare, Pedra opened her steno pad and held her pencil ready. *Thank you, God,* she quietly prayed, *that the stroke didn't take away his speech. He has so much wisdom to offer. I hope I can do it justice as I take down his words.* She loved this routine of listening to his stories, then when he'd need to rest, typing her notes into a growing computer file.

As soon as he was settled in the bed, Frank jumped right in:

The next few years after Marcie's death were dark ones for me, with the only light being my son. At first, I didn't think much about my childhood dream, or how to see Christ in others. I was treading water, trying to survive my sorrow. I alternated between ignoring God and barraging Him with my pain. Eventually my old habits resurfaced, and my attempt to see Jesus in others brought me back to a healthy relationship with Him.

I began to teach at a Catholic grade school during the day and focus on Daniel the rest of the time. He was my little buddy, and for the first few years didn't cause me any worry. Maybe he sensed I couldn't have handled it. But the fog began to lift from my mood over time, and just when I thought I could be happy again, he started to draw away from me. He attended the same school where I taught, but he preferred that the other students not know we were related. That was hard. I felt like he was ashamed of me. And I was so proud of him!

He was one of the popular kids in his classes. He had the kind of personality that made friends easily. He was on every sports team of the season and played ballgames with the others the rest of the time. He loved the basketball hoop that my dad had installed on our driveway back when he had hopes I'd enjoy the game. Dad would have loved Daniel and been so happy to attend his games. Daniel still went to Mass with me most mornings, our special time together.

Frank paused to shift in the bed. Pedra handed him his ice chips and water, and after a sip, he continued.

My experience with the homeless, or unhoused as we call them now, and my other service work, had taught me how few things a family really needs. That was the crux of the new discord between Daniel and me. He wanted what his friends had. Computers were becoming common in households, and he loved playing computer games with his friends. We, on the other hand, didn't even have a television! My dad's old black and white one had died years earlier, and I never replaced it. And sports shoes! He wanted whatever the famous basketball stars endorsed, but they were twice the price, or more, than simple serviceable shoes. And his feet just kept growing!

I didn't make much as a schoolteacher. We were blessed to have my parents' three-bedroom house, which kept expenses low. Yet, even if I'd made more, I'd have wanted Daniel to learn the value of simplicity. I can't imagine the Child Jesus not being satisfied by what Joseph could provide Him. I was trying to teach gratitude. Daniel thought I was being selfish.

And my students made life difficult, also. The girls had their cliques, and the boys had their tricks. I spent many hours trying to impart lessons of kindness and Christ-like behavior. I hope I made a difference in their lives. I'm afraid I wasn't at my best, but I did what I could to see Jesus in each of them—and in their parents. They were even harder to please than the children. When I was a student, parents had more respect for teachers, and always assumed any complaints about their children were justified. But times had changed, and now many parents weren't open to the idea that their children had made bad decisions.

But back to Daniel. As he graduated eighth grade and moved on to high school, he spent less and less time at home and more time out with his friends or playing on teams. I went to every game I could and hoped that it meant something to him, even though he'd never admit it.

Though he gradually stopped attending morning Mass with me, claiming he was too tired, he went through Confirmation training and anointing. Pride filled my chest to see him stand before the bishop and profess his faith. So, it hit me extra hard when he stopped even going to Sunday Mass with me. I tried to force him, but I knew deep down that would only make it worse. The world was calling him away from me and away from our faith. I prayed all the harder for him. I still pray for him today!

But the story I have to tell you next is a complicated one. I'm going to nap for a while now. Maybe you could check on me after lunch.

∞

Pedra stood and gathered her things. She wondered about Frank's son. Did he live too far away to visit? Were they estranged? She stopped at the nurse's station and asked, "Does Frank ever get any visitors?"

"Besides you? You're very dedicated to him." The nurse smiled. "He does get one other visitor. Bishop Raymond comes in every Sunday evening. He must be a pretty special friend for the bishop to make that much time for one old man."

So, no family then. No Daniel to hold his father's hand as he lay getting weaker and weaker. She tried to assume the best of his son, but she couldn't help judging him.

She and Frank were more alike than she had realized. Neither had loved ones in their lives.

∞

In the afternoon, Pedra peeked in, and Frank gestured for her to enter. He said they were going to start him on physical therapy in an hour, so he began his story immediately.

I'm going to tell you about the night God refreshed my faith, but Daniel lost his. His friends called him Dan by then, and he didn't want to be Daniel anymore. But it's the name Marcie gave him, and I wanted him to be known that way. Another point of contention for us that I probably should have let go.

In Daniel's senior year, he was on the football varsity team enjoying a winning season, and he had a girlfriend named Cindy. I worried about them getting too intimate, of course, but as far as he knew, I had gotten his mother pregnant while she was a junior, so what example was I? Maybe how not to do things. But when I got to know Cindy, I worried less. She was levelheaded and wanted to make something of herself, so I hoped that would keep them safe.

I was more worried about his teammates. I'd heard rumors about heavy drinking after games, so I didn't allow Daniel to go anywhere after their competitions. He hated that, of course, but hadn't rebelled yet. We only had one car, so I'd drop him off, watch the game, and then drive him home. One Saturday, he asked if he could have the car after the game to take Cindy out for her birthday. We decided he could drive me home and then go pick her up. Unfortunately for him, or maybe fortunately, I saw her father in the bleachers and sat with him. He mentioned how Cindy had been home in bed for a couple days with the flu. I realized Daniel had lied to me, so when we got to our driveway, and Daniel thought I'd give him the keys, I told him what I knew. He got out of the car, slammed the door, and started walking down our street. I followed him, trying to talk sense into

47

him, while still holding firm on punishment for his lie. We stood face to face in the street, both angrier than we'd been in a long time.

Suddenly, a car came careening around the corner toward us. Daniel had his back to it and was focused only on his anger. I grabbed him by the jacket, pushing him as hard as I could out of the way, and shouted, "God, save my son!" He was bigger than me by that age, but I firmly believe God gave me extra strength. I succeeded in getting him out of the path of the car, but it hit me and threw me into the air. I don't remember anything after that, until a few days later when I woke in the hospital, so the rest of the story is from my son.

He called 911, screaming for ambulances, not only for me, but for several members of his football team who were in the car, which had hit a tree after hitting me. I learned he stayed at my side at the hospital, terrified that I would die. And maybe it was touch-and-go for a while there. I had broken a hip and two ribs and lay in a coma.

According to my son, he railed against God, demanding why He'd let this happen to me. Wasn't it enough that he didn't have a mother? Would God take his father, too, a father who, in his words, had served God so diligently? Well then, he reasoned, if I died, he didn't want to have a God that was that mean. He'd never have faith in God again. He was determined not to believe.

By the third day, things weren't looking good for my recovery. The doctors had started trying to prepare him for the worst. Terrified, he realized he needed a world where miracles were possible. He needed a God who could heal. He made a pact with God to return to his faith and become a priest if God would spare my life. Soon after that, I awoke.

That timing, that answer to prayer, was more than a healing for me. It worked miraculously in Daniel's heart and soul, too. Little did I know that when I begged, "God, save my son," He would save him spiritually as well as physically.

Five key players of the football team were hurt badly enough to be unable to play for weeks. The coach decided to forfeit the season, partially as a lesson to the whole team about underage drinking and driving, and about making choices to promote one's health. With his newfound time,

Daniel immersed himself in his faith. True to his word, he returned to our daily morning Masses. He studied the Bible. He joined the Youth Group and would tell his story to anyone who would listen. He began to research colleges with seminary programs. He'd found his own Savior, and more importantly, his Friend. He admitted to being pretty fond of me, too, and happy to have me safe.

Frank was grinning. "It was one of those holy instances that you remember for the rest of your life," he said. "I'm sure you have some of those, too."

Pedra shrugged. "I'll have to get back to you on that," she said, but knew being assigned to transcribe Frank's story would be among her holiest of moments. She looked at her watch and realized she should return to the convent. First, she gave Frank a quick kiss on the cheek. They both grinned, and he waved her goodbye.

∞

As Pedra arrived at the convent and passed Mother Superior in the entry, the woman quietly said, "Please come talk to me in my office."

Feeling like a child in trouble, Pedra followed her and tried to calm her drumming heart.

"Take a seat, Postulant Pedra."

She sat across the desk from the older woman. The office was small and austere. Mother Superior was a believer in simplicity. Her conversation manner was direct. "I've been watching you, Pedra, unsure of whether we were the right place for you. I had almost decided we aren't, until I saw you interacting with your sister postulants the other night. I had been hoping for that kind of progress from you. It seems you usually spend as much time as possible alone. We are a group of women intentionally choosing to live in community to support each other in our faith journey. That said, I haven't yet decided we are the wrong place for you."

"Thank you, Reverend Mother." She stammered the first words, but then calmed herself with a deep breath. "I'm trying to figure this out, too. My time with the patient Frank is really helping me, I think."

"I'm glad to hear that. I don't see you as a nurse in the future, but it seems we've found a niche that suits you, at least for now. Bishop Raymond has expressed his pleasure." She paused thoughtfully. "I heard about you helping in the ER with sign language. I had no idea you were fluent. I'm wondering what else we don't know about you." She waited expectantly but Pedra didn't respond.

"Certainly, you are full of surprises. You may go. We will talk more soon."

"Yes, Reverend Mother," Pedra said as she stood and left.

Behind her she heard her superior mumble, "Shorthand and sign language. Interesting."

Chapter 9

The next day, Pedra arrived carrying flowers from the convent garden. "I knew something was missing in this room, but it took until now to figure it out." She set the vase on the wide windowsill and then settled into the chair beside Frank's bed. Usually, he started storytelling as soon as she was ready, but today he stayed silent. She tilted her head, waiting.

"You have a question," he said.

It amazed her how good he was at reading her. "Tell me more about your son," she said. "Did he become a priest?"

Daniel did enter the seminary after high school. And this might be a surprise for you—I did, too!

We chose different directions. He wanted to be a Jesuit priest, attracted to their emphasis on education and intellect. I, on the other hand, considered joining the Franciscans. I'd always been drawn to St. Francis of Assisi's simplicity and love for nature. But back to Daniel. I had been putting money away from each paycheck for him to go to college, but I hadn't planned on us both paying tuition at the same time. So, I taught for a couple more years before I entered the diocesan seminary, having felt called there, rather than to the Franciscan monastery. I figured I'd have more in common serving parishioner families, rather than living with men who'd never experienced marriage and fatherhood.

I considered selling the house but wanted to be sure Daniel wouldn't change his mind and need a place to live. However, his vocation was true and survived the ups and downs of his college studies and summers in service to parishes. I ended up giving my house to the bishop to be used for whomever needed it short term. It has seen a series of immigrants, some unhoused people, a few seminarians from Africa, and several single mothers who needed time to get back on their feet.

We used to joke that it took me 20 years of adulthood to come around to being a priest, but that God came out ahead because he got two for the price of one. I started my studies later than Daniel, but already had my bachelor's degree, so finished well before him. Jesuits often study for twelve years or more before being ordained. I would have liked being ordained the same day as my son, but I was a priest a good five years before him. I was given an assignment as an assistant to a superb pastor at a parish not far from here. I learned so much from him. I didn't have to struggle to see Jesus in him. He was one of those men who relates to the priesthood commitment as a shepherd to his flock. He had strong faith, a servant's heart, and a healthy work ethic. I couldn't have asked for a better first assignment.

Meanwhile, Daniel's leadership aptitude was recognized, and he was sent to Rome for additional studies. What a wonderful opportunity! I was so happy for him. While Daniel was in Rome, he wrote to me often. He learned about the history of the Church and the inner workings of the hierarchy, while I blessed pets on the Feast of St. Francis and baptized white-gowned infants. He was frequently in the presence of cardinals, and I was frequently in the confessional with the heart-broken and spirit-weary. We were both right where we were meant to be, right where our gifts were most needed.

Eventually, I was made pastor of my own parish in another town, and I loved my flock dearly. I easily saw Jesus in them. I saw Him reaching out to them. I felt tenderly toward the man in the front pew who struck his chest gently each time Jesus' name was spoken. Or the woman who sat across the aisle from him so that her four young children could see well, though tending to them probably meant she didn't get to pray much herself. Of course, some folks made it harder to see Jesus. Some parishioners complained constantly about noisy children, Mass times, the music, or what the lectors *wore. A few disagreed passionately about every topic brought up at the Parish Council meetings.*

I was lonely at first. I missed Daniel terribly, and knowing how far away he lived made it worse. It reminded me of how I felt when Marcie left. I knew she was doing wonderful service somewhere for the poorest of the poor, but I desperately wanted her to be with me. And I desperately wanted to be close enough to Daniel to at least see him for coffee now and then. I tried to offer it up as a sacrifice. Some days were harder than others.

However, for the most part, I was happy being a priest. I loved officiating at weddings, watching the bride and groom gaze into each other's eyes. Yet, their happiness in being joined as one emphasized how very alone a priest is. Whenever I felt especially sorry for myself, invariably some sweet family would invite me to dinner. The children would play their newest pieces on the piano, or sing for me, or ask me to join them in a board game, and I'd drive home that night feeling so thankful. God had reminded me that I wasn't alone, and that He had me under His wing.

I did attend Daniel's ordination in Rome, feeling both proud and humbly grateful at the same time. Eventually, Daniel returned to the States. He taught theology at a Catholic college for a while, then led the theology department, and eventually became dean. We made it a point to see each other whenever we could, and at least one week a year we got away together for vacation. Bishop Raymond was truly kind to us that way. He and Daniel were golf buddies, so that might have helped.

"And you," Pedra asked, "how did your ministry progress?"

"This afternoon. Come back this afternoon and I'll tell you more about my priesthood. I think I need a rest first before Physical Therapy."

When Pedra returned after her lunch in the cafeteria, he continued right where they had left off.

One of my favorite blessings as a priest came with the honor of listening to someone's confession. You might be surprised at that, but sharing such a sacramental moment with anyone is a gift. Sometimes people come in during scheduled hours, and you can tell they want to get in and out as quickly as possible. But most people, once they've said what they need to say, are open to the many graces God wants to shower on them. And the people who make an appointment for confession off-hours are often hungry for such grace and any spiritual counseling that I'm moved to offer.

Many people come to the confessional weighed down by guilt and feeling bad about themselves. I listen, not for my own knowledge, but as a conduit connecting God and the parishioner. Their words, both the penitent's and God's, flow through me, and I am both humbled and awed by how the Spirit directs my response to them. You'd think after so many years as a priest I'd be used to it, but I still often wonder, did I just say that? Where did that come from? It certainly isn't my own wisdom, but that of the Spirit. Being used that way, for the healing of a sorrowful soul, is one of the greatest gifts of the priesthood!

I don't want the person to leave weighed down by what they've just told me. I want them to realize what a blessed child of God they are, so there's a question I've always loved asking people before I give them their penance and send them on their way. I say, "Tell me when you've been most like Jesus." Well, usually they start telling me about when they've been the least like Him, when they've missed the mark. You know, the Hebrew word for sin is often translated like an arrow missing a target or falling short. But that's now what I want them to focus on. So, I interrupt and gently say again, "Tell me when you've been most like Him."

I hear truly humbling answers.

One woman said, "When I overlook my husband's little irritating idiosyncrasies and just love him as he is."

Another said, "When I'm up in the middle of the night with my infant, and she's crying, and I'm exhausted, but I cuddle her and sing to her and rock her until she falls asleep. That's what Jesus must long to do with us when we aren't behaving. So often we misbehave because we are tired or hungry or don't feel loved. But He's right there holding us and loving us through the tough times."

Great truth rests in that wise young woman's words. But women aren't the only ones who are Christ-like. One man told me, "My joints hurt *most of the time. I've had severe arthritis for years, but I try not to complain. I think about Jesus and how He suffered for me, and I thank Him, and then the pain doesn't seem intolerable."*

One man had a hard time letting go of focusing on occasions he'd missed the mark. I had to repeat my question several times, but finally he looked up at me with tears in his eyes and said, "I'm divorced. I didn't want it, but I am, and sadly, my ex-wife is truly angry with me, so she belittles me in front of the kids. I'm most like Jesus when I resist the temptation to do the same about her. He never returned anything but good for evil. I try to remind myself of that, and I try to tell the kids about her good qualities. I want them to know that whatever part of them that comes from her isn't anything but wonderful."

I really identified with that man. I tried so hard not to be critical of my Marcie, especially to our son. I didn't always think purely loving thoughts, but I tried not to ever express them to Daniel.

After a thoughtful pause, Frank asked, "How about you, Pedra, when have you been most like Jesus?"

Pedra looked up from her notepad, then looked down again, not wanting to meet Frank's gaze. She could feel her cheeks burn, and her first thoughts were all the ways she wasn't like Jesus whatsoever. Frank let her relax into his silence and simply waited. Finally, she said, "I'm most like Jesus when I'm in this room with you, listening to your stories, and completely enjoying being with you. I hope He enjoys being with me. I am absolutely sure He enjoys you, Frank."

"Pedra," Frank answered, and she was aware of him wheezing a bit, "you have no idea how wonderful you are. I might not have much time left to convince you, but you are. You make me feel like there's nowhere else you'd rather be. That's a remarkable gift of friendship. And I promise you, Jesus loves being with you, listening to you confide in Him, sharing your friendship. He loves you, Pedra. Just the way you are right now. He doesn't need you to be perfect. He'll aways encourage us to be better, but

He also delights in how we are right now."

She looked at the good man through tears in her eyes.

"Go home," he said. "Talk to God. Listen to Him. Let Him show you all the ways you are wonderful. Tomorrow is soon enough to tell you more about my priesthood."

∞

That evening in chapel Pedra talked to her newfound Friend, for the first time realizing she was loved, no matter how imperfect she felt. Instead of seeing herself as a plain person with an ugly name, she pondered Frank's assertion that she was wonderful in special ways. A warmth filled her chest, and tears came to her eyes. God loved her! Not because she was trying to be a nun. Not because of any reason other than that she was His. A daughter with one Father who loved her. She realized, suddenly, that she was enough. She was loveable. And in realizing her worth, she planned to somehow share God's love with others. She didn't know how, yet, but a beautiful seed had been planted and took root.

Chapter 10

Bernard was 30 miles from Daniel's city on a quiet highway when he came around a turn and was the first to arrive at a serious two-car accident. He pulled over to park on the shoulder and jumped out of his car. He could hear a child's frantic cry and that drew him to the car with a little girl of five or six, with dark hair and eyes, buckled in a booster seat in the back. He fumbled with straps until he had her loose and then nestled her close to try to calm her. When she had quieted some, he realized she was pointing to the driver, presumably her mother. Mom did not look good. Her face was drained of any color except for a large bruise growing on her forehead. Still holding the child in one arm, he dialed 9-1-1 and reported the accident, though was a little unsure of his location. The area was new to him, but he could see huge grain elevators near the highway and that seemed to help the emergency operator locate him.

She said she would send two ambulances and asked how the occupants of the second automobile had fared. Bernard hurried to the other car, which, judging from the damage, must have hit the child's car head-on. The driver had been thrown through the windshield and lay several feet away. Bernard told the child in his arms to close her eyes, but she didn't, so he gently covered them with his hand. She buried her head into his shoulder. He moved closer to the person and could smell alcohol. His shirt was wet, and a beer bottle wasn't far from where the badly twisted man lay.

Presumably the drink had spilled during the crash. There'd be no breathalyzer test, as the man was no longer breathing. Bernard reported his condition to the operator, then scanned the road and shoulder area to be sure no one else was thrown from the car. No other people were inside the car either, so he returned to the child's mother. She was groaning, which he took as a good sign. At least she was alive. The operator had told him not to move her unless absolutely necessary.

He expected the child to be crying for her mother, but she didn't say anything. She leaned toward her mother with her arms out, but Bernard kept hold of her, partly to comfort her, and partly to keep her safe along the roadside. A second car stopped, and the driver identified herself as a doctor. He told her what he knew about the two drivers, and she hurried to the mother to see if she needed care. Soon ambulances arrived. They asked the child if she was hurt anywhere but she didn't answer. It was only then that Bernard realized she was using sign language. How he wished he knew what she was saying! He spoke several languages fluently and many more passably, but he would have traded them all to be able to communicate with this little girl.

The EMTs tried to take the child from him, to transport her in the same ambulance as her mother, but as they lifted her, she screamed, and she clung to Bernard. "I'll come with her, and hold her, if that's ok," he said, and they allowed him to ride with them. He waited until they had loaded the mother in, then he noticed her purse and took it with him. Maybe the authorities could use it to find someone with whom this poor child would feel safe. When the ambulance started up, Bernard jumped at the sound of the siren. The little girl did not. As they pulled away, he saw a stretcher being lifted into the other ambulance, with a sheet drawn over the man's body and face.

∞

Soon after Pedra sat down in Frank's visitor's chair, a nurse burst into the room. "Oh good, you're here," she said. "We have another need for you in the ER if you're willing. A little girl is using sign language, and we don't understand. Her mother is... well, could you just come right away?"

Pedra glanced at Frank, who nodded, and she stood to follow the woman. "I'll be back when I can," she told Frank.

"I'll think of a story to make it worth your while," he answered.

Following the nurse at a near run to the elevators, Pedra tried to quiet her own nerves, in order to be ready to calm a child. Hurrying made that difficult, so once in the elevator she took a couple of deep breaths. "Tell me more?" she asked. "I'm Pedra, by the way."

"Becky," the nurse offered, then continued. "The little girl and her mother were brought in by ambulance a few minutes ago. Bad car accident. The mom is unresponsive. The girl might have a broken collar bone but can't answer our questions. At least, not that we can understand."

The elevator dinged and the doors opened into the Emergency Room waiting area. Pedra followed the nurse through the admission doors and to a curtained examination space. She felt unnerved by the number of people working on the mother, the beeping monitors, and the crying child, who clung to a man's chest. No wonder the little one was sobbing. The scene was scary, even for an adult. The others made room for Pedra to approach the little brunette, who was maybe six years old Pedra guessed, and whose brown eyes were wide with fear.

Pedra signed, "Don't be afraid, little one. I can help you talk to the others, and we can get your questions answered. What is your name?" She assumed the man was the child's father and wondered why he wasn't helping her communicate. Maybe he was in shock.

The girl's fingers flew to spell out S A R A H. Her breathing calmed a little.

"Hi, Sarah," Pedra signed and smiled. "My name is P E D R A. Can you tell me where you hurt the most?"

Sarah pointed to her chest over her heart and signed, "I hit the straps hard. This was my first ride out of the little kid car seat and in a big girl booster. Is my mom okay? She won't look at me."

Pedra was vocalizing the girl's responses, and she looked now to the team to see if anyone could answer the child. Becky, the nurse who had come to get her, responded, and Pedra signed her words to Sarah. "Your mom is unconscious, or kind of sleeping, and we are going to do everything we can to help her… and you."

Sarah nodded and then looked at Pedra again. "I'm scared," her hands said.

"I know," Pedra signed back and said aloud, "but we are here to help. Is this your dad who is holding you?"

"No," she replied. "He's a stranger but a nice one. He helped me out of the car and has been holding me ever since."

Pedra looked at the man, who seemed shaken but trying to be brave, and smiled at him. "He's obviously a nice stranger," she signed to Sarah. "Is there anyone we can call to come be with you and your mom?" Every instinct made Pedra want to draw the girl into her arms and enfold her with a hug, but even that act of comfort wasn't possible because of her injury and the man holding her.

"My daddy just died; he was our only family," Sarah signed, and the emotion that wasn't possible to voice showed on the little girl's face. "We were driving back to where we lived before he got sick."

"What happened to him?" Pedra asked.

"Mama said…" She paused. "He was really sick, but I don't know how to spell what he had. He was in a hospital a long time."

A pediatrician entered the room and Pedra focused on helping her communicate with Sarah. They lifted the child from the lap of her "nice stranger" and used a wheelchair to take her to

Radiology for X-rays. Pedra held her hand between signing what was happening. When they had decided her collarbone wasn't broken, only bruised, Pedra expected to return her to her mother's bedside and the man who had been holding her. However, a nurse said the woman had been taken to surgery and the man had moved to the waiting room.

"What will happen to Sarah now?" Pedra asked.

Looking through her purse, the nurse and Pedra learned the mother was Vivian Johnston. The address on the driver's license was out of state. It would take time to track down any relatives.

"We have a call in to Child Protective Services," the nurse said. "CPS will try to find someone who knows sign language for her to stay with for now."

"I'll take her," Pedra surprised herself by saying. She didn't know what was next, but she knew it was right. "Can you ask them if she can stay with me until they find family?" Somewhere in the last two hours, her heart had connected with little Sarah, and an innate maternal instinct had bloomed.

"But you're a sister. You live in a convent," said the nurse.

"I'm a postulant. I haven't made any vows, and I'm not sure what vocation God is asking of me. I can look after her until other relatives are found. I want to love her and take care of her. What do I need to do to make that happen?"

"I'll call CPS and ask. I'd guess they'll send someone to meet you."

∞

When Sarah was given pain medication and a bed in the pediatric ward, it looked like she would fall asleep soon. Pedra taught the child how to ask the nurse to notify her when she woke, using the sign for rock, bumping one fist onto the other. "Rock," she said. "My name, Pedra, means rock in Spanish." She let the nurses know the sign and then when Sarah had fallen asleep, headed to Frank's room. As she passed through the ER waiting room, she saw the man who had been holding Sarah.

He stood. "How is she? How is her mother? I haven't heard anything."

"Sarah is asleep and probably will be for quite a while. She's exhausted and possibly still in a bit of shock, but no broken bones. I know her mother was taken to surgery, but I haven't heard anything more. If you want, I can take your number and let you know when I do."

"I'd really appreciate that!" he said with a grin. "I'm Bernard Lovejoy, and you are?"

"Pedra Clump," she said, wishing again that she had any other name.

"Pedra, you were wonderful with Sarah. I'm so glad they found you. How scary for her not to be able to hear or be understood. I love that you know sign language."

"Actually, today, so do I!" She took his card and promised again to let him know when she learned more. *What a kind person,* she thought as she headed toward Frank's room.

∞

A doctor was talking to Frank, so Pedra waited in the hallway. As the doctor left, he stopped, looked at Pedra, and said, "Maybe you can convince him to have surgery. A pacemaker may help his fibrillation. Chances are good it would extend his life by several years. But if he won't agree, his next 'episode' could be his last."

Pedra didn't want to intrude on Frank's decision, but she had quickly come to love the man and hoped he would consider the surgery. She thought of Sarah's mother and guessed that if she had any chance at living more years, the woman would seize the opportunity. Pedra had heard the low murmurs in the ER. Sarah's mother was unlikely to survive. And Pedra could foresee she would need to break the sad news to Sarah. Yet there was always hope. That woman had someone to live for. Maybe Frank did, too.

Pedra entered the room, and her face must have told Frank what she was thinking, because he said, "Don't start. I know the doctor talked to you in the hall. He probably wants you to talk me into the surgery."

When Pedra didn't answer, he continued, "A pacemaker is a possibility, but you see, at any moment another stroke could take me. And I've lived a good long life. I don't have family left, and the people who were my parishioners before I worked overseas have probably forgotten me by now. I've fought the good fight and run the good race. Maybe God is ready for me to go be with my loved ones. Maybe I'm ready for that as well."

"But your story isn't finished," Pedra answered. She meant the story of his past that she was honored to hear, but she also meant the story of his future. The man was a wealth of good will and wisdom. The world still needed him. She realized *she* still needed him.

"What about Daniel?" she asked. "You said you don't have family left. What happened to Daniel?"

"That's a tale for another day. I'm not feeling up to that one yet. But don't leave. I want to hear more about the ER. Were you able to help?"

She sighed, then told him about Sarah and her mother. She shared about Bernard's kind help with Sarah, and how he gave her his number so she could tell him when she learned more. "I think he's one of the good guys," she said before she paused. "What will happen to Sarah if her mother doesn't survive? Where would she go after she's discharged? She needs family who can communicate with her."

"Is it possible that you two need each other?" Frank suggested.

Pedra tilted her head, wondering at his confirmation of her own thought. How could she, currently a postulant living in a convent, take on a child? Yet, the idea excited her. She had already started to love the girl. It seemed profoundly right, much more than joining the convent had. She could almost sense her soul rejoice at the idea. Is this what a leading from God might feel like?

"How could that work?" she said aloud, though it was more the beginning of a plan than a question for him. "I don't have a home I can share. I gave up my work and my income when I entered the novitiate. I don't know anything about raising a child or helping her heal from such a great loss."

"If this is God's will, He will take care of the details," Frank answered. "You just need to try to follow what you think He wants, and then let Him make straight the path."

"Could this be how you felt when you received the letter from Marcie asking you to marry her?"

Frank nodded. "I was scared and excited but most of all I wanted to do anything I could to help her."

"That's how I feel right now!"

"I can see it in your eyes. This is how following a call should feel. Yes, it's a little frightening, but more than that, it's exhilarating. It just feels right." He had caught her excitement.

Pedra considered his words, which led her to ask the question she had wanted to ask since the first day she met Frank. "I think I'm more connected to the spiritual side of me now, after feeling such a leading to help Sarah, but still I wonder, how can I see Jesus like you do?"

Frank nodded as if he'd been waiting for her to ask.

"First," he said, "it helps to ponder how much He loves you by realizing what He endured for you." He settled into his story-telling mode, and she resumed taking dictation.

"Just listen, don't write," he said, and she laid the pencil on the page.

Imagine that you've just awakened from surgery. You had needed a heart transplant to stay alive and someone had given you their loved one's heart. You had thought you only had days to live, but now a whole future opened up for you. You'd want to know about that donor. You'd want to express your gratitude to their family. That's very much the feeling we should have as we ponder Jesus dying to give us a new heart of love, a new chance at redemption. Dying so that we, you and I, could enter a new life and live forever with God.

We should, as we realize what a gift we've been given, want to know all about our Donor. Let me help you know Him better.

Imagine yourself as Jesus, sitting side-by-side with your best friends on Holy Thursday. You've just instituted the Eucharist as a way to stay with your friends, knowing that you'll be physically leaving them later tonight. You've taken them away to pray, and you plead for strength from your Father to get through what lies ahead. You pray for your followers, the men and women whom you've been preparing for three years. You pray, desperately wanting to find another way, any other way, but already it has begun, and you bow to your Father's will. One of your chosen twelve has betrayed you and led the Romans to arrest you. The soldiers come to take you to your judgment and your death. Your followers have scattered, none remaining at your side. You are stripped, beaten, scourged, and perhaps even worse, you've heard your Peter, your rock, deny you.

Frank took a deep breath before he continued.

Dragging a heavy, rough-hewn cross along your final sorrowful way, on a shoulder still raw from the whip, you see the pain in the eyes of the women. You see your mother and are pierced by the same grief that pierces her heart. You are nailed to the cross, your hands and feet bearing the weight of your body on the excruciating pain of the nails. You struggle to breathe, knowing you are counting your last gasps. But you summon breath to give your mother to John and by so doing, make her mother to the world. And then you forgive the people who've inflicted the pain that is unbearable, so unbearable that you die.

If imagining yourself as the suffering Jesus has moved your emotions, you have just glimpsed Jesus.

Now imagine yourself just as you are, trying to be His follower, but place yourself kneeling at the foot of the cross. You look up at Him, the One you hoped would ease your pain. And instead, He has just exhaled His last breath.

Fear. Doubt. Grief.

If you have known any of those emotions, any of this pain in your life, you have been at the foot of the cross and you have seen Jesus through suffering. More importantly, He has seen you. He knew then, and He knows now, the pain in your heart. Whether it is emotional pain from abuse, betrayal, abandonment, guilt, or the physical pain of a broken body as yet unhealed, He saw you from the cross. He sees you now. And He knows that in long nights of anguish, or brief awareness of His nearness, you have reached out to Him. You have found Him through pain. Perhaps seeing you, as you looked with faith to Him, eased some of His suffering.

Frank shifted in his bed and reached out with his left hand to pat Pedra's.

We are truly blessed to live many years after that crucifixion day. We know the hope of the resurrection—both Jesus' resurrection and our own still to come. In that hope, we see Jesus, and not only see Him, but we are invited to live beyond the pain, to live with Him forever. Through Easter, we will see Him in joy! He sends us experiences of joy to keep us filled with hope.

Perhaps we experience His touch of joy in nature. Something about green trees, untamed animals, water on the move, snowy mountains, or a star-teemed sky can make our hearts surge with thanksgiving to the Creator. Leaving routine behind as we travel into the wilderness holds restoration for the weary. Jesus exemplified this by going away to pray. He calls us to retreat to the desert, as well as to mountaintop experiences. "Beside still waters He refreshes my soul."

We might experience Jesus' joy through children. Holding a tiny baby and seeing one of her first smiles delights us. The miracle that we behold, as we snuggle a newborn, is a taste of the miracle of taking Jesus into our arms and loving Him with awe and thanksgiving. Watching a child discover new experiences refreshes our own outlook. Having a little one come running for comfort and being calmed with a hug or soothed on our lap lifts our hearts. Rocking a child to sleep brings peace to our hurried lives. Seeing a teen discover pride in a job well done, we share their joy. Giving a son or daughter away to a well-chosen spouse gives us hope for the future. Holding a new grandchild, we relive holding the parent. Such happiness!

We can also find Jesus' joy through helping others. There's an old Chinese proverb, "If you want happiness for an hour—take a nap. If you want happiness for a day—go fishing. If you want happiness for a year—inherit a fortune. If you want happiness for a lifetime—help someone else." You've done that for me, Pedra, and I thank you. Which brings me to another route to joy, gratitude. Appreciating what we have, we focus on how blessed we already are.

You will discover these joys of nature and children and service and gratitude as you help little Sarah.

We best experience Jesus and His joy as the result of love. Simply love, Pedra. Love Sarah. Love everyone who crosses your path.

Pedra left Frank that day feeling her life was full of new possibilities, and her soul was somehow more alive than ever.

She hurried to Sarah's bedside wanting to share her joy.

Chapter 11

The next morning, Bernard Lovejoy was shown into Bishop Raymond's office for his appointment and introduced himself as they shook hands. The room wasn't opulent like Bernard had expected, but struck him as simple and efficient, which put him at ease. After he'd taken the chair the bishop indicated across the desk, Bernard told him about his search to find his half-brother, Daniel Roma, whom he believed had been ordained a priest. He watched the man's expression run from surprise to sadness and then to animation.

"If you're willing," the bishop said as he stood, "come with me. There's someone you need to meet."

∞

Frank had just greeted Pedra and waited while she settled into her dictation chair, when the bishop knocked and entered Frank's room, followed by a red-haired man in his late 30s or early 40s. Something seemed familiar about him to Frank, though he couldn't have said what.

"Frank," Bishop Raymond said, "I'd like to introduce you to Bernard Lovejoy."

The two shook hands and, after an awkward pause, the bishop said, "Bernard came to see me this morning. He had been doing research on your son Daniel, which led him to me."

The men certainly had Frank's attention now, and he turned to Bernard. "Why were you researching Daniel?"

Bernard seemed agitated, and his eyes swept from Frank to the bishop, to the window, briefly back to Frank, and then to the floor. "I'm adopted. I didn't find out until recently when I did a DNA test. Since then, I've been trying to find my birth family. The DNA test suggested that Daniel Roma, your son...?"

Bernard paused, and Frank nodded.

"Your son seems to be my half-brother. I've been trying to find him to meet him." He lowered his voice and again studied his shoes. "I was hoping to talk to him, to find out more about who I am. I never dreamed I might find a father though."

"How old are you?" Frank asked, his voice strained.

"I was born in 1984."

"What month?" Frank sounded almost desperate now.

"May."

"Dear God," Frank said, and it sounded more a prayer than an oath. "Your hair is the same shade of red as hers. And you have Daniel's eyes. I see it now." Tears ran down the old man's cheeks. "I didn't know about you. I'm so sorry. We could have shared a life together, you, Daniel, and I. How could she do that to us?"

"Please," Bernard said, "I don't follow you. Tell me what you mean."

Frank wiped away the tears and took a deep breath. "Yes, you must be my son. Your mother was my wife, Marcie Roma, and your brother was Daniel. She left us in November 1983, a few months after Daniel was born. She must have been carrying you by then. I don't understand why she didn't tell me. I'll never understand why she didn't stay." He shook his head in disbelief, then lifted his left arm inviting a hug.

Bernard hurried to the edge of the bed, sat, and embraced the father he'd not expected to find. "Dad!" he said, and his voice cracked.

"My son," Frank sobbed.

Pedra sneezed and regretted the attention it drew. "Excuse me," she said quietly. Neither the bishop nor Bernard had noticed Pedra, as her chair was behind the door they opened as they entered.

Frank straightened saying, "Oh, I'm so sorry. I didn't mean to be rude. Bernard, this is Pedra, my friend, who is writing down my life story. Pedra, this is my son, Bernard!"

Bernard, Frank's son. Bernard, the kind man who'd held Sarah all the way to the hospital.

"Hello again, Bernard," she said at the same time that he exclaimed, "Pedra!"

"You know each other?" Frank asked.

Pedra explained about meeting Bernard the previous day, then stood, asking, "Should I give you some time to catch up? I can come back later."

But just then a nurse hurried in. "Looks like we need to calm down, a bit, Frank. Your pulse is setting off warnings." She turned to the others. "I'm sorry, can you give Frank a break? Maybe come back one at a time a little later?"

All three nodded, said, "Of course," and made their way into the hall.

"Tell him my story, Pedra!" Frank called.

"There's a cafeteria we could visit if you'd like to eat something or have a cup of coffee," Pedra offered.

The three made their way to the basement cafeteria and, though the bishop ordered a coffee, Pedra and Bernard each bought a glass of milk. "I haven't met anyone else who drinks milk on a break," Bernard said. "I'm too much of a nervous person for caffeine."

"That's funny," said Pedra, "I thought I was the only one."

When they'd all sat down, Pedra said to the bishop, "I thought I had it all figured out. I figured you were Frank's son

Daniel and had maybe changed your name at ordination. That would explain both why you visit and why his son doesn't."

"I wish you were right," the bishop answered. "I'd be honored to be Frank's son. But I'm not, nor am I as brave a man as Daniel. I visit Frank because Daniel can't, and I'm the reason why he can't."

The bishop looked from Pedra to Bernard. "I'll tell you about Daniel now, Bernard, but I wanted to introduce you to Frank first to soften the sad truth about your brother. After ten years as a priest, Daniel came to me. I wasn't his Jesuit Superior, simply his friend, but he told me that he wanted an assignment where he could truly help people. He wasn't satisfied passing on his immense theological knowledge to a new generation. He wanted to serve the poorest of the poor, like Mother Teresa—Saint Teresa of Calcutta—did, or, as Daniel said, 'Be down in the trenches with those who are struggling.' Those words gave me an idea. I suggested he look into being a military chaplain. I'd received a request from the Army for a Catholic chaplain who would be willing to go overseas with a battalion that was due to deploy within a month.

"I told him about that request and his whole face lit up. 'I'd be able to finally do something like my mother,' he said. His mother...." he nodded to Bernard, "and yours... had given her life to help in Africa when AIDs had begun to kill so many. I guess that had left an impression on him, even though he never knew her. Personally, I have to admit I judged her for what others saw as selflessness. She had abandoned him and his father, after all. In my opinion, his father was the real hero, raising the boy by himself, and doing an impressive job of it. Daniel had grown into an intelligent, yet kind, man. And if he'd wanted to become a parish priest like his father, I'd have had no objection. In fact, that's what I should have suggested first. Parish priests are definitely down in the trenches with our struggling flock."

He looked at Pedra. "I know I don't need to convince you

what a good man Frank is, not if you've been listening to him tell his story. Daniel couldn't have done better than to emulate Frank. But the adventure of my first suggestion had already worked its way into his heart. I couldn't convince him otherwise, and his Superior gave his permission. So, a month later, two of our best priests, father and son, said goodbye to each other, and Daniel left on his way to a foreign desert. He had only been there about a month when his Jeep hit an IED—improvised explosive device— and was disabled. He threw himself over the young man who'd been driving him and took the bullet fire that followed. He saved that boy's life, no doubt, but he died doing so."

The bishop laid his hand on Bernard's shoulder. "I'm sorry. I'm sorry to have dashed your hope to meet your brother. He was a hero."

Bernard nodded and Pedra could see tears in his eyes.

Checking his watch, the bishop stood. "I'm afraid I must be on my way to a meeting," he said. "Bernard, can you find a ride back to your car, or would you like to come with me now?" He stood, and the others did, too, out of respect.

"Oh, I'd much rather stay, but thank you. You've given me a lot to take in and staying here sounds like a good idea. I'll visit with Pedra and then go see Frank again. I'll make my own way back. Thank you so very much, Bishop Raymond. You've given me a father."

"Then I know at least two happy men, today," the bishop answered. "Pedra, I'll leave them in your care."

Pedra and Bernard talked for about an hour, with Pedra telling him the parts of Frank's story she assumed he'd want to know. She'd been struck by Bernard's eyes when she first met him, and tried several times to decide what color they were. However, Bernard never kept eye contact for long, and by the time he stood to return to Frank's room, she still wasn't sure if they were hazel or green.

Pedra headed to spend time with Sarah. Bernard had agreed

to meet Pedra again the next day for their milk break, and she found herself looking forward to it more than she expected. There was something vulnerable about Bernard and his nervous attempts at socializing that made her see him as a kindred spirit.

Chapter 12

"How did your time with Frank go?" Pedra asked the next day when she'd met Bernard at the cafeteria again.

"I think the word "surreal" best describes it. We had a great talk, with Frank— um, Dad—filling in more of the story that you started. I was devastated to learn of Daniel's death, of course. I'd been anxious to experience having a brother. I was raised an only child."

"I was, too," Pedra said. "It leaves a bit of a hole in one's life, doesn't it?"

"Indeed. I'm not sure someone who hasn't experienced it could understand. I mean, it's great to grow up having so much attention and being the center of your parents' lives, but it's a bit lonely, too. And it doesn't help one learn how to relate to other children. That can make school hard."

Pedra nodded her agreement, though her own childhood felt less cherished than Bernard's must have been. And watching him now, she could imagine his nervous mannerisms might have secluded him, much like her late talking did to her. Without thinking about it, she laid her hand on his to stop him drumming his fingers. He misunderstood her intent and took hold of her hand. She didn't want to pull it away, but she felt confused. Trying to act naturally, with her hand being held by a man for the first time ever, she asked, "What do you do for a living, Bernard?"

"I teach languages in high school. I love the idea of

communication, and that has driven me to learn as many as I can. I'm on break now and decided to spend the summer finding my birth family, if possible. And I have!"

"Do you live here?"

"I live across the state, actually. But I really like what I've seen here. Now that I've found my dad, I've been thinking about moving, if I can find a job."

He motioned to the steno pad she was carrying. "I saw you writing in that when we were in Dad's room yesterday. He says you're transcribing his life story. May I see it?"

Pedra felt a little reluctant to give the tablet to him, but she did, and his eyes widened as he paged through it. "What is this? It's like code, or a foreign alphabet?"

"It's just Gregg shorthand. It used to be quite common for secretaries to take down dictation with this but it's a dying art nowadays. Technology has made it less necessary."

"This is so cool!" Bernard's words sounded like a teenager, and his enthusiasm made Pedra chuckle. He paged through and shook his head in wonder. "It's another language! Can you read me some?"

Pedra took back the notebook and read some of what she'd transcribed two days before.

"Cool," Bernard said again. "Do you speak or write any other languages?"

Though it wasn't something she usually told people, she felt a little proud as she said, "Just shorthand and ASL, American Sign Language." He already knew that from when she helped Sarah, so it didn't feel like boasting.

"You are fascinating!" said Bernard, and Pedra could feel her cheeks warm.

"Oh, I've made you blush! I'm so sorry. I'm not used to talking to women much outside of work and even then, I do as little as I can. I'm on the Spectrum."

"I don't know what that means," said Pedra.

"I have some autistic traits. I'm quirky, or sometimes I seem awkward because of it. I talk fast and more than I should, so I have to try to hold myself back some. But autism also gives me some special abilities, 'my superpowers,' my adoptive mom used to say. I learn languages very easily and hear accents and can imitate them. Some people with autism are great with math or science but my ability is communication. You know two languages that I've never learned. I'm going to have to fix that! I want to at least learn ASL."

Pedra found herself thoroughly enjoying Bernard, in spite, or maybe because of his quirks. He was so open and accepting of himself. That was something she'd like to learn from him.

"Oh! I haven't asked you about your life." Bernard made eye contact, and he carefully said, "Tell me about yourself, Pedra. What do you do for a living?" It sounded rehearsed but his facial expression told her he really wanted to know.

Pedra found herself not wanting to tell him she was discerning being a religious. "I live in community with other women," she said. "The others are mostly nurses, and I definitely don't have that ability. I guess my "superpower" is listening and writing about people. That's what I'm doing for Frank. Bishop Raymond asked me to, and I've certainly loved this assignment. Frank's such a good man and could teach the world so many things. He has spent his life trying to see Jesus in everyone he meets and in every situation he encounters. I'm sure right now he is praying fervently in gratitude for you finding him."

Bernard looked down, then glanced quickly into Pedra's eyes and back down again. "Is he dying?" he asked softly.

Pedra didn't know how to answer. What would it be like to find a father you didn't know, only to learn he might not have much time left? She sighed. "It's possible, I think," she said. "But there's always hope. And it's truly a gift that you found him before he's gone."

"I was too late with Daniel," Frank said.

"I would have liked to know Daniel, too. I've only known

Frank for a brief time, but he has already made an amazing difference in my life."

"He says he didn't know about me, and I believe him, but why would his wife, my mother, do that?"

"You heard she left Daniel with Frank when he was only a few months old. Frank says she wanted to go help those who needed her more, though I can't imagine leaving my child, if I had one. Certainly, Daniel needed her. Maybe she discovered she was expecting you after she left, and was afraid to go back, or to burden Frank with two babies. From what Frank says, she didn't have a good mother to be an example to her. I'm sorry she put you up for adoption."

"It wasn't so bad. I didn't know until recently, after all. And my parents really loved me. They were older, so maybe they'd been waiting for a child a long time. I had a good upbringing. I guess in some ways I should be grateful to her for that."

"That's a good way to look at it. I can tell you're Frank's son, just from that sense of gratitude, and looking for the best in people or situations."

"Thanks, I'll take that as a compliment, since I know how much you admire him. I still can't quite get over that my birth dad is a priest. And what about Daniel? Why is—was—he a half-brother?"

"That's probably a better question for Frank than for me."

She stood. "I want to check on Sarah before I go back to Frank. You should have more time alone with him, anyway."

As she walked toward Sarah's room, she remembered Frank's words, "Love everyone who comes across your path." She wondered if that might mean Bernard, too.

∞

Sarah was sleeping, so Pedra transcribed more of Frank's story into her laptop. Then she headed for Frank's room. As she walked in, Frank's heart monitor started to alarm. "No!" he groaned. "Not yet. I'm not ready yet."

"No! We aren't finished!" cried Pedra. She met eyes with Bernard, who looked frightened.

Already a team was rushing into his room with a crash cart. Pedra stepped out but heard him say, "I'll have the surgery. Call the doctor. There's something else I need time to do."

Pedra prayed to Jesus, who knew her, and who knew suffering.

∞

A kind-looking woman with graying hair approached Pedra while she and Bernard waited for Frank's surgery to be over. "Pedra Clump?"

Pedra stood and nodded.

"I'm Grace from CPS. I've been told you'd like to provide emergency foster care for Sarah Johnston. Am I right you hadn't known her before yesterday?"

"Yes. Somehow, she stole my heart almost immediately. I know I'm not experienced and that it would be ideal if she could be with family, but I'm willing to do anything for her for as long as she needs me."

"We've done a background check—your fingerprints on file with your application to work for the hospital speeded things up—and not found any problems, but I'm told you live at a convent. How will that work?"

Pedra glanced at Bernard, whose eyes widened. "I'm just a postulant, that's like a questioner, and I've been suspecting convent life isn't right for me, anyway. I'll leave and find another home for us. I have some savings. We can stay in a motel until then. I have secretarial skills. I'll be able to find work quickly." She hoped that was true.

"Well, it's not ideal, but we haven't found anyone else

available who knows sign language. And our search into her home address isn't turning up any leads, either. I can't promise this will be long term, maybe her mother will surprise us all and survive, but fill in these forms and if all goes well, we will grant you temporary guardianship for now. You'll need to attend some training sessions, and we will want to do a home visit when you're settled. But let me say, thank you for being willing."

Pedra didn't know she could feel so many emotions at once. She was delighted to have permission to take care of Sarah, but she was frightened for Frank's sake, and nervous about the talk she would need to have with Mother Superior very soon.

"Be sure we know your contact information at all times." Grace said. "I'll give you my card. Is this number your cell phone where you can be reached?"

The number was correct, and the efficient Grace was quickly on her way again. Trying to also be efficient, Pedra left a message asking Mother Superior to come talk to her in the surgery waiting room when she was available.

Within minutes, the Reverend Mother arrived bustling from her office on the first floor, and Pedra stood to greet her. "Postulant Pedra, I'm hearing bits and pieces of possibly momentous changes in your life. Please catch me up to date." They sat down together in a corner away from Bernard, and Pedra told her about Frank's surgery and then about Sarah and her mother.

"I think I'm being called to help this child. I'm frightened of the responsibility but also very excited about it. If her mom doesn't survive, I'll need to leave the convent in order to pour myself into her care."

"I've never seen you so animated, Pedra," Mother Superior responded, "not even when we told you we had accepted you as a postulant. I think you may be right about this call. You have my permission to pursue it, and also my consent for you to return if you find God leading you back to us. Follow the joy!" She stood. "Now, I need to get back to our hospital work, as that is *my* calling.

God bless you, Pedra!"

∞

A half hour later, Pedra was still in the surgery waiting room when she was paged over the intercom. She hurried to Sarah's bedside in the pediatric ward. The little girl looked relieved to see Pedra and reached out for a hug, which Pedra returned very gently.

"I woke up and Mama wasn't in the bed next to me anymore. Where is she? Is she okay?" Sarah signed frantically.

"I'll find out. I'll be right back," Pedra's hands responded.

Pedra hurried to the nurses' station, only to learn that Sarah's mother had passed away. Staff had found that her driver's license denoted that she wanted to be a donor. Her body was now being prepared for several transplants.

"Including her heart?" Pedra asked, but she already knew the answer to her real question. She wished Frank could be a recipient, but his stroke and weakness probably didn't make that a likelihood.

"Yes, she is giving gifts of life and function to eight different people as we speak," said the nurse with profound respect in her voice. "We paged you, hoping you could help our social worker tell little Sarah."

Pedra got advice from the social worker and then turned to walk back to the little girl, a heart-rending responsibility immediately ahead of her.

∞

Pedra watched Sarah smile as she and the social worker entered her room. The knowledge that she must deliver news that would break the child's heart weighed heavily on her.

"Where is my mom?" Sarah signed.

Pedra sat on the bed and drew Sarah onto her lap, both

facing each other so they could see the other's hands.

"I'm very, very sorry, Sarah," Pedra said and signed. "Your mama has died. I believe she is in heaven now with your daddy, and they both are sending you so much love. They will be watching over you always, and I know they wish they could be with you." She glanced at the social worker, who simply nodded and didn't offer any more words.

Pedra studied Sarah's eyes, but the child didn't cry, so Pedra continued to sign, "Your mama was what they call an organ donor. She had a note on her driver's license that said if she died, to give her eyes to someone who was blind, her heart to someone whose heart wasn't working well, and other body parts to people who needed them. She's providing wonderful gifts to people who will have better lives now. She was so generous."

Sarah tilted her head, as if to understand better.

"Can she give me her ears?" the child's hands asked.

The question wrenched Pedra's heart. "No, I don't think so. But I promise to do everything I can to help you hear, or to help you communicate in whatever way is best."

"Who will I live with?"

"Have you remembered any family?" Pedra chastised herself for hoping not. Surely the child should be with family members who loved her, rather than with a stranger, even if the stranger had begun to cherish her.

"I don't think so. We were always alone for holidays. My daddy was a soldier, so we moved around a lot. I don't remember any family besides my mama and daddy."

"I want to take care of you," said Pedra. "I want to help you any way I can. I met with a lady earlier today who is in charge of where children go when they can't be with their parents. I asked them to let me be your guardian. That's a person who fills in for your parents. If you want, I have permission to take you to live with me."

"You're nice. I think I'd like to live with you. I mean, if I can't live with Mama and Daddy."

Tears rose in Pedra's eyes, her heart touched by the little girl's trust. She asked, "How are you feeling?"

Sarah touched her chest. "Where my heart is still hurts, but not as bad. I feel a little scared and a lot of sad."

"I haven't ever been a mom, but I'll do the best I can. You can tell me if I do anything wrong, okay?"

"Okay," answered Sarah's hands, and then, "I'm not going to see my Mama or Daddy again, am I?"

"Someday, when you go to heaven, which I hope is a long time away still."

"Heaven sounds like a good place. I'm glad Daddy has Mama with him. I wouldn't want him to be lonely. But I'll really miss them."

"Yes, I know you will. And that's okay. And it's okay to cry and be sad. Sad things have happened to you. But I'll be nearby to help. Now I think you should try to sleep. Tomorrow, or when the doctor says you're ready, we will leave the hospital together and start a new adventure. Now, how do you like to be tucked in?"

"Don't make the sheets too tight, and always lean over and kiss me after you pull them up. That's what Mama did."

She followed Sarah's instructions and then stayed at her bedside until the child slept again.

∞

Pedra was finally allowed into Frank's recovery room and found Bernard at his side. He told her the surgery had not gone as well as they had hoped. Frank had suffered another stroke during the procedure.

"I'm so sorry," she said to Frank, who lay in the bed very pale, but awake. "I wanted to encourage you to have the surgery. We all thought it was the answer." She told them about Sarah's mother passing and being a donor. "I wish you could have been the recipient of Sarah's mother's heart. I told the sweet child about the gifts her mother is giving people even after she has died."

"I'm not sorry," Frank said weakly. Frank's words came interspersed with pauses. "Her heart will go to someone ... who will live a long life with it. ... The pacemaker allowed me enough time to give a gift to you and to her daughter. ... As soon as I was awake after the surgery, ... I talked to the bishop and ... was able to finish what I needed to do."

"A gift? I don't know what you mean," said Pedra, looking from Frank to Bernard for clarification.

"Bernard says he doesn't need any financial help, ... so we asked the bishop to give you and Sarah my parents' home. ... That will make it possible for you to care for the child. ... And I asked him to find work for you. ... You weren't meant to be a nun, I'm guessing, ... but God has great plans of service for you anyway. ... I can see you interpreting for the deaf, ... or transcribing stories for the dying. ... I can see you being a wonderful mother."

Pedra couldn't believe what she was hearing. "I don't know what to say, other than how deeply grateful I am. I have learned so much from you." She looked at him through a welling of tears. "I love you." Bernard came to her side of the bed and put an arm gently around her shoulder. She thought of Sarah, who had not yet cried for her mother, yet Pedra couldn't hold back tears for this new friend.

"You know," Frank said, "I've been blessed by the women in my life. ...I had a good mother, a wife I loved very much, ... and friends like you. ... For priests, ... our mothers remain the most cherished women in our lives ... until they pass. ... And for those of us whose mothers passed when we were young, ... the Blessed Virgin becomes our surrogate mother, and we honor her deeply.

"I've been especially blessed ... because I met the Virgin Mary personally when I was seven. ... She's been dear to me ever since. ... Your mother, Pedra, died and is watching over you from heaven, ... and so is Sarah's mother. ... But the Blessed Virgin

Mary is as well, … and she can intercede for whatever you need. You and Sarah, and you, too, Bernard, will be fine."

Frank looked into Pedra's eyes and again seemed to read her soul.

"You have a question?" Frank wheezed. A nurse came to check Frank's vitals. She frowned a bit, and then attached an oxygen mask over his nose and mouth. She watched the monitors again, nodded, and left the room. Frank's breathing improved, and he could speak more smoothly.

"I do," Pedra responded with hesitation. "So many."

"Might not have many more chances. Shoot."

"What's your full name?"

"Put your pencil down first." She had opened her steno pad out of habit.

She set down the pencil.

"Father Frankincense Mudd," he said, and then struggled for a deep breath.

Bernard let an "Oh dear!" escape.

She couldn't believe it, and she couldn't help herself. She grinned.

"I've always hated my name," he admitted. "So, I just tell people Frank." He looked from Bernard to Pedra. "Please make sure they don't put the whole name in my obituary."

She promised, and then replied. "I hate my name, too. Pedra Clump. I'm a pile of rocks." She giggled. It seemed they were meant to be friends.

"You know, Pedra, or Rock, is a name to be proud of. …St. Peter was one of Jesus' closest friends and the 'rock' the Church was built upon. …We could call you Rocky. …Or Pete." He laughed and that made him cough.

"I kind of like Rocky." She hurried on, so he could take a break from talking. "I was just thinking that frankincense was one of the first gifts offered to Baby Jesus. It's symbolic of healing, sacrifice, and holiness. Much like you, I think."

After a moment simply enjoying each other's unfortunate names, and the other's assertion of their name's significance, Father Frank took another deep breath of oxygen. "You have one more question?"

"I'm sorry if this is insensitive."

He motioned her to go on.

"Are you afraid of dying?"

"Oh, heavens, no! After almost a whole lifetime of striving to see Jesus in every person, and in every situation, it will be delightful to not have to struggle. He'll simply be there, face to face with me, and I know what He'll look like. His face will beam joy at me, and mine will respond likewise. He loves me in spite of my faults. I've spent most of my life in obedience, doing what I can of His work here on earth, but I truly can hardly wait now. And I have loved ones in heaven expecting me."

He smiled. "Lately I've been seeing Jesus' joy through gratitude for all He's done for me throughout my life. Two of the things I'm grateful for are you, Pedra, and you Bernard. I do wish we'd had more time."

"I don't want you to go," Pedra said with a sob.

"Dear friend, we will see each other again in the next life."

He looked to Bernard and reached out a hand to his son. "God wants us to love and to laugh, spreading His joy wherever we go. That gave me another idea, but only if you like the thought. A lawyer is coming today to settle some things for me. What would you think if I legally changed my last name to Lovejoy? Then we'd match, father and son."

Bernard grinned. "I'd love that!"

"You couldn't have chosen a more appropriate name," said Pedra.

∞

After his dear friend Pedra and his (thank you, Jesus)

newfound son had left the room, and after a brief meeting with his lawyer, Frank settled into a deep sense of prayer. He had so much to be grateful for. *God is good, God is love*, he thought. He began a wordless mindfulness of gratitude and praise. His breathing difficulties and the pain he hadn't told anyone about drifted away.

Frank felt someone sit on the side of his bed, and he pulled himself back to consciousness. As he opened his eyes, he chuckled with joy.

"Hello, Frank," the beautiful woman said. "You'll see my Son very soon, now."

"I've been waiting for a long time."

"I know. I've been right here all along. So has my Son."

"Of course you have. Thank you for that. Thank you both for my whole life."

Mary took his gnarled and shaking hand, "Frankincense Lovejoy, shall we go?"

Chapter 13

He passed away that night.

Pedra received word at the convent. She assumed Bernard was also called. She'd like to offer him her condolences but didn't know where he was staying and wanted to do it in person, not by text.

She still went to Frank's room to visit early the next day, as she had every day since this wonderful assignment, but the empty bed was too much for her. She wept from the anticipation of missing him so very deeply. When she could, she wiped her eyes, making herself visualize him where he surely was now, rapt with Jesus' joy, enveloped in a hug. She was seeing her friend with her "faith eyes." As she rested in the image, two more people emerged in her mind, their arms around Frank in a loving embrace, and Jesus' arms around them all in a group hug. Frank looked up and directly at Pedra. "Rocky," he said with pride, "these are Marcie and Daniel." They all smiled at her, and Marcie and Daniel together said, "Thank you." Then they turned their attention back to Jesus.

"Goodbye, Frank," Pedra whispered. "You were one of the good guys."

Jesus looked into Pedra's eyes and soul. He smiled.

∞

When her tears had stopped, Pedra stood, ready to leave

this hospital room for the last time but looking forward to having Sarah at her side when she left the building. Just then, Bishop Raymond knocked softly on the door and came in. "The nurses told me you were here. I want to thank you for the time and patience you've given Frank."

"Truly, I should thank you. I've loved every minute of getting to know Frank. I can't believe it's over. He taught me so much in such a brief time."

He nodded as if he, too, felt blessed to have known Frank.

He cleared his throat. "I sent his son to his death."

After another throat rumble and a sniff, he continued. "So, since then, I became a surrogate son to Frank. It was the least I could do. I'm no replacement, but I visited, and we remembered Daniel together, and I think it gave him some pleasure."

"Daniel's death wasn't your fault," Pedra ventured. "He wanted to go. And you brought Frank another son!"

Both were silent for a moment.

"Why didn't he have any other visitors?" Pedra asked. "Surely a pastor like Frank would have dozens of parishioners coming to pay their respects."

"That may have been my doing, also. You see, I asked Frank to hear my confession once, years ago. I learned what a gifted confessor he is. You probably haven't gone to confession to him, but has he told you about his question? He asks when we've acted most like Jesus."

"Yes, he asked me. I was a deer in headlights, not knowing whether to freeze or flee."

"I felt the same way," the Bishop continued. "I settled for saying 'when I shepherd my people.' Frank nodded and replied, 'Yes, we ministers try to emulate the Good Shepherd. We try to lead our flock along safe paths, to protect them from dangers, and to anoint them with healing oils when they are hurt. We may need to fight off wolves or go seeking the lost. And we certainly endure a shepherd's loneliness as we watch over them.' In those words, he summarized all the ways, as a bishop, I should be a shepherd and, at the same time, all the ways I know I've failed. That wasn't his goal, I'm sure, but ever since then I've been a better bishop, I hope." He paused, and Pedra waited for him to say more.

"Shortly after he heard my confession, I learned that the sites of Marian apparitions often seek confessors who speak English, for the many pilgrims who journey there. I mentioned it to him, and he jumped at the chance. I think he needed a change after Daniel died, and the travel suited him like an adventure. I hope I made the right choice to send him. Certainly, our diocese lost out on a wonderful priest. But know this, Pedra. People all over the world will mourn his loss once they know. He blessed many lives with his gifts of listening, encouraging, and advice."

After they shared a quiet moment, the bishop continued. "The strangest dream came to me last night, and I've felt better since. In my dream, I watched Frank being hugged by Jesus, and then the two were joined by Marcie and Daniel. The latter two looked directly at me and said—"

"Thank you," interrupted Pedra. "I had the same... vision."

The two smiled at the gifts they'd been given: the heavenly image they'd shared, and the friendship of an exceptional man who saw Jesus.

The bishop handed her the keys to Frank's house, saying the most recent tenants had moved out just a day or two ago. He invited her to come talk about a job after she was settled.

"I'll send you the file when I've finished transcribing his story," Pedra said.

"And I'll make sure to send it out to the world. Bernard would say we all need to learn to see Jesus: in churches, in suffering, in nature, in joy..."

"And in ourselves and each other," Pedra added.

"There'll be a funeral?" Pedra asked.

"Yes, tomorrow at the cathedral at ten o'clock. I hope I'll see you there."

"I wouldn't miss it," she answered.

Chapter 14

Sarah was discharged into Pedra's care. Together they walked to the convent to gather the meager possessions that were Pedra's. She began to mentally list all the things she didn't own that she and Sarah would need in their new home. She sent heavenward a prayer of gratitude for Frank and his wonderful gift. The other sisters were kind to Sarah, and to Pedra, too, as she said goodbye to them, and they wished her well. Though they hadn't grown as close as Pedra knew they should have, they were as close to family as she'd known for many years.

As the two left the convent, they discovered Bernard waiting for them just outside his car. Pedra hurried to him, and surprising them both, set down her suitcase and hugged him. She stepped back to look in his eyes. "I'm so sorry, Bernard, that you didn't get more time with Frank."

He nodded and looked down, then took a deep breath and said, "I thought you might need a ride. I pictured you with more things to carry." He took the one small suitcase from Pedra.

"That was really nice of you to think of us. I don't own much anymore, but I appreciate you saving Sarah from exerting herself with a long walk." She glanced at Sarah and saw a little look of infatuation in her eyes as the child reached out and took Bernard's hand.

"I bought a booster seat for you," he said to her. "I

remembered you had one in your car." Pedra translated his words into sign.

Sarah looked away into the distance, and her face fell.

"I'm so sorry," Bernard said. "I've brought up a horrible memory for her."

Pedra knelt down in front of Sarah, and the child released Bernard's hand, so her hands were ready to communicate.

"I remember the accident," Sarah signed, and Pedra voiced for her. The child looked up at Bernard. "And I remember how you held me and made me feel safe. Thank you. Thank you for helping me and trying to help my mama."

Tears filled Pedra's eyes, and when she looked at Bernard, she saw the same in his.

"Let's go see our new home," Pedra said and signed. They all needed a distraction.

Bernard cleared his throat of emotion. "I hope you don't mind me coming along. I know Dad's things won't be there, but I'd love to see where he lived so I can imagine him there with Daniel."

"Of course I don't mind. The house really should be yours. You might also feel connection with your grandparents, Frank's parents, because it was their house first."

Bernard lifted Sarah into his arms, hugged her gently, and then buckled her into the booster seat. Pedra was touched to see his tenderness toward the child, but made herself focus on the process, wanting to learn how to do the straps and keep Sarah safe in case they bought a car. Then Bernard walked to the passenger side, and held the door while Pedra got in. The gesture made her understand Sarah's sense of safety around Bernard. He was the type of man who watched for ways to help. Pedra hoped she could learn that skill as well.

When they had driven to the house and parked in the driveway, Pedra opened her car door, but Bernard hurried around to hold it for her. Then he unbuckled Sarah and the three, looking every bit like a family, stood and studied the little home. It was old, but well cared for, and boasted the steeply pitched gable roof, half timbering, and tall windows of a two-story Tudor home. It was painted a dark blue, Pedra's favorite color, with white brick porch pedestals and chimney. A chimney meant a fireplace! She'd always wanted a fireplace.

Pedra pulled the keys out of her pocket and unlocked the front door, feeling like she was entering a fairytale cottage. The other two followed her into a small hallway that offered the options of a stairway straight ahead, a small living room on the right with a well-worn blue sofa and love seat, and a dining area on the left with a table and chairs for four. Beyond the dining room, a small galley kitchen shone with a recent cleaning. Pedra opened cupboards to find them fully stocked with dishes, pots and pans, mixing and storage bowls, silverware, and a few small appliances, like a toaster and a mixer. The refrigerator held two gallons of milk, as well as eggs and the makings of peanut butter and jelly sandwiches. It felt like Christmas!

Behind the kitchen and the living room, two small bedrooms and a bathroom completed the first floor. The beds looked welcoming, made up with sheets and comforters. The room with a bunkbed was obviously set up to be Sarah's, and the child ran to hold the doll that waited on the bottom bunk. Someone had gone to great lengths to prepare the house. She remembered that the home had been used by the diocese, thanks to Father Frank, for temporary housing for immigrants, houseless people, single mothers, and others in need. She realized there must be a committee who prepared the home for each new set of occupants. Pedra raised another prayer of gratitude.

Together the three climbed the stairs to a third bedroom, and Pedra felt she could almost sense Frank in the room as a child.

"He lived here," Bernard said, reverently.

A half-sized door was locked, but it opened with another key on the same ring the bishop had given Pedra. In a small attic they found two boxes, one marked "Frank," and the other, "Daniel." Inside Frank's box they found a framed photo of a red-haired young woman with a bouquet in her hands, nestled against a younger version of Frank. "This must be their wedding photo," Pedra said, and handed it respectfully to Bernard. "Your mother," she whispered. Below that photo were several more that they presumed were Daniel at different ages, and one of an elderly couple, probably Frank's parents.

"You should keep all of these," Pedra said to Bernard, and he nodded his appreciation.

Sarah wandered out of the attic and sat on the floor to play with her new doll in Frank's old room.

The second box contained report cards and yearbooks, along with a letterman's jacket. A photo album held high school photos of friends and sports teams. One picture showed Frank in a wheelchair outside a hospital with a grinning Daniel ready to push him. The final pages displayed a handful of postcards from foreign countries, with one or two lines about her volunteer work and signed "Love, Marcie." At the very bottom of the box rested two framed photos – one of a smiling Frank in his black priest outfit, and the second with Frank's arm around Daniel, both wearing their clerical collars and grinning. On the backs were written, "First Ordination," and "Second Ordination."

"I'd like to hang this one of Frank on a wall," Pedra said, "and I think you should keep this one of the two of them."

"My dad and my brother," Bernard murmured as she handed it to him.

∞

Back downstairs in the room that would be Sarah's, Pedra opened the dresser drawers and found 3 or 4 outfits in each of two sizes, one of which would surely fit Sarah. *How kind!* Pedra thought. In her own room she found two dresses in the closet, as well as a gift card on the dresser to the local St. Vincent de Paul used-clothing center. The hospitality committee had thought of so many of their needs. For tomorrow though, Pedra's black jumper would serve her well enough at Frank's funeral.

"I'll be right back," Bernard called as he opened the front door. Within a half hour, he had returned with a child's meal and two hamburgers from the nearest fast-food restaurant. Best of all, were three chocolate milkshakes. Pedra hadn't tasted one of those since before she entered the convent. She wasn't sure if her smile or Sarah's stretched wider.

"What a treat!" she said to Bernard, while Sarah ran and hugged him around the legs.

"May I always be able to make you two so happy, so simply," Bernard said, and Pedra found herself liking the idea of Bernard's 'always.' Then she sobered. He didn't live here. He had a job a few hundred miles away. After the funeral, there'd be no more reason for him to stay.

Chapter 15

The funeral was not at all the tiny, quiet service Pedra expected. When she arrived at the church with Sarah and Bernard, who had picked them up that morning, there were already dozens of men dressed in black and wearing clerical collars, visiting with each other near the entrance of the cathedral.

"So, he did have people who knew him," she whispered to Bernard.

"I'm guessing every priest in the diocese is here," he answered.

Pedra, Bernard, Sarah, and a few others comprised the non-clergy attendees, at least until all of the sisters from Pedra's convent arrived together and sat behind them near the front. She turned to smile her appreciation at them and once again realized they were very much like family. Sarah had brought the doll that she found on her bed and played with it soundlessly. Bernard had made the sign of the cross, genuflected before entering the pew, and now knelt in prayer.

He must be Catholic, Pedra realized, and the thought made him all the dearer to her. They had that in common, at least. A woman walked to the altar and stood at the lectern to welcome them. The organ began to play, and the cantor sang, "I will raise you up, on eagle's wings." The three stood and Pedra and Bernard joined in. Bernard had a very pleasing voice, Pedra thought, then turned her attention to the sung prayer.

A simple wooden casket was rolled up to the front of the aisle. Behind it, men's voices filled the church as the priests processed two by two. They divided left and right into the front pews. At the end of the procession were two priests wearing white vestments and Bishop Raymond, who would preside. When the song ended, the bishop welcomed everyone and began the Mass of Christian Burial.

Sarah signed that she needed the restroom. Pedra realized she hadn't thought about taking care of those needs before Mass. She had so much to learn about mothering. She and Sarah walked quietly out by the side aisle and found the restroom near the entrance. They returned by the same route and Bernard welcomed them back with a smile. The bishop was giving a sermon about seeing Jesus in all our circumstances and in everyone we meet, as Father Frank had exemplified in his life. When the Mass was finished, the bishop invited anyone who had a story about Father Frank to come to the microphone. Several priests talked about going to confession to him, or receiving sought-after advice that changed their lives. Some spoke of Daniel, or Father Roma, as they called him, and how highly he had spoken of his father.

A reception followed in the church hall next door. Nearly everyone who had attended the Mass also came to the hall for sandwiches and coffee. Many of the priests stopped by the table where Pedra sat with Bernard and Sarah to offer their condolences. Mother Superior hugged Pedra before leaving, as did several other sisters. The younger ones eyed Bernard and Sarah before looking at Pedra with grins and raised eyebrows. She wondered how much they knew or what they were surmising. Yet, looking at the two seated on either side of her, and fully aware they had not known each other two weeks earlier, she certainly could imagine herself part of a family.

The last person to come to their table introduced himself as the Army chaplain from the base where Sarah's dad had been assigned. "Hello, Sarah," he said, but she was playing with her doll.

Pedra touched her and pointed her attention to the chaplain.

"I'll sign for her," Pedra said.

"I'm sorry, I forgot she couldn't hear me." He knelt down to be at Sarah's eye level. "Sarah, I'm so sorry to hear that both your mom and dad have passed away. I've come to arrange..." He looked at Pedra. "At the hospital they told me I'd find you here. I don't know how much Sarah understands, but I've come to accompany her parents' remains back to the base where they'll be buried. We will have a service there that we invite you to attend. And I'm afraid we will need someone to move their things from their apartment. Would that be you?"

"I guess it would. I've been assigned Sarah's temporary guardian until they can find family, and I'm planning to adopt her if they don't."

They exchanged contact information and, before the chaplain left, he asked, "Was today's service for someone else the poor child loved and lost?"

"No, this loss is ours," she motioned to Bernard and herself, "we are the ones who loved and lost him."

All too soon, it was time for the burial. Pedra felt grateful to ride with Bernard to the cemetery and to stand near him at the graveside. He reached for her hand and his touch warmed her heart. Frank's resting place lay among many other priests who had served the city over the years. As the casket was lowered into the ground, she and Bernard leaned toward each other until their shoulders touched. The group of mourners was small now, only the bishop and the three of them. When the final prayers were over, she repeated, "We are the ones who loved and lost him."

∞

After the cemetery, Bernard offered to drive to a grocery store so Pedra could stock the kitchen. He even insisted on paying, though she had some savings to get them through until she had a paycheck. Together they unloaded the bags of food into the cupboards and refrigerator. "How are you going to manage without a car?" he asked, his face full of concern.

"I found a bicycle in the garage," Pedra answered. "I'll add a child seat to the back and a basket to the front, I guess. Or maybe a trailer. God's taking care of us. I just know it will all work out."

"I should head home," he said, "maybe tomorrow."

The idea of not seeing Bernard again made Pedra's stomach clench. She had enjoyed playing family but had to realize it couldn't last. "Yes, I suppose you need to get back to your home."

Sarah tugged on Pedra's jumper. "What did he say that made you sad?" she signed.

"Bernard needs to go back home. It's far away."

"No!" Sarah signed with angry hands. "Too many people have gone away!" Then, haltingly, as if afraid of the answer, "Are you going to leave, too?" At that moment, the tears that the child had held back burst forth like a waterfall over a cliff.

Pedra drew Sarah into her arms, assuring her that, no, she wouldn't leave. She'd be with Sarah for as long as she needed.

Bernard had listened as Pedra spoke what she signed. He looked down, and his, "I'm so sorry," was barely audible. After he had recovered his composure, he raised his head. "Thank you, Pedra, for all you did for Dad, and for how kind you've been to me. I wish I..."

He hugged her instead of finishing his sentence, then tried to hug Sarah but she pulled away from him. He hurried to his car, and they watched him drive away. Pedra wanted to stay strong for Sarah's sake, but she could easily have joined her tears to the child's.

Chapter 16

A week after Bernard had left, Pedra and Sarah parked a rented car in front of the military apartment that matched the address on Vivian Johnston's driver license. The complex was on an Army base and, though well maintained, looked very plain.

"That's my home!" signed Sarah, and she tried to unbuckle herself from her booster seat.

"Let's go see it then," said Pedra as she helped release the child. She had been given a key by the Army chaplain, whom they had stopped to see first, and now she unlocked the door.

Sara ran through each room and signed, "Mama?" When she returned, she looked at Pedra with fresh grief at the realization that her mother wasn't there. Her fingers explained, "I knew she wouldn't be here, but I guess I still hoped."

Pedra drew her into a hug and then signed, "Let's see what is here that you'd like to take back to our house."

They wandered through the little two-bedroom apartment. Sarah picked up a stuffed gorilla and hugged it. "Its name is Koko," she signed. "Like the real Koko gorilla who learned sign language."

"Well, Koko definitely needs to come home with us," Pedra responded.

They emptied the clothes drawers in Sarah's room into boxes and Pedra carried them to the car. Another box was soon filled with books and one more of toys. Together they ventured into the bedroom Sarah's parents had shared. The little girl opened the closet and hugged a sweater of her mother's, inhaling deeply. "It still smells a little like her," she signed.

Pedra located some photo albums, wondering if she'd find any hints about Sarah's extended family, but there were only pictures of the three of them. Sarah's father looked young, but handsome in his uniform. Pedra collected more framed photos from the dresser top, including one that must have been Sarah as a newborn.

They had left the front door open, and someone called, "Hello?"

Pedra caught Sarah's attention and pointed to the door. The child's face lit up! Her fingers flashed M A N D Y! And she ran to hug the young woman who knelt down to embrace the child.

"Hi," Mandy said to Pedra, "I live next door. Is it true? Has Vivian passed away? We heard so, but hoped it was wrong. First Marco and now Vivian, it's just too much, isn't it?"

Mandy scanned the living room, now devoid of anything personal. "I'll be right back with tea," she said. "I'm sure we have lots to ask each other."

She returned with steaming mugs and brought her daughter, a year or two younger than Sarah. "You girls play while we talk," she said, and though Sarah couldn't hear her, this must have happened often before, because the two disappeared into Sarah's room.

Pedra told Mandy about the car accident when Sara and her mom had been driving home after Marco's death in the hospital, and how she had asked to take care of Sarah when Vivian passed away. Mandy told Pedra about Marco's fight with cancer, and how he'd been flown to a bigger hospital, hoping for a cure. When he died, Vivian and Sarah, who had joined him at the hospital, were expected to return to the base and gather their things to move out. They hadn't come back, and Mandy had been waiting to know what happened to her friend.

"Do you know if Sarah has any family?" Pedra asked.

"Not that I've heard of. Of course, we become substitute family to each other on base, but no, no one ever visited, and I don't remember them talking about anyone. They mentioned once having met at an orphanage."

Pedra wasn't surprised. The social workers had contacted the military but there was no record of relatives.

"How is Sarah taking her loss?" Mandy asked.

"You know, she's doing pretty well, given the circumstances. She gets teary now and then, I think when a memory surprises her. But she will start school in the fall in a special program for Deaf children. I think that will help both of us connect with the Deaf community. Then I'll start a job that is waiting for me that is flexible enough I can be home when she is. And we are looking into what we can do for her, either with hearing aids or cochlear implants. The future looks promising."

The two talked of the kinds of things mothers talk about, and Pedra felt like she had found her path. She was a mom, with normal worries and stories, and she loved being right where she belonged. Mandy helped carry boxes to the car. The two exchanged contact information. Sarah hugged her little friend when it was time to go, and kissed Mandy on the cheek. Pedra had permission for the two to sleep in the apartment that night.

The next day they attended the memorial service for Sarah's father and mother. Several people stopped to hug or speak to Sarah afterwards. Pedra signed their words to Sarah, who was showing signs of emotional exhaustion. She brightened some when Mandy and her daughter hugged her.

"What is left for you to do here?" Mandy asked Pedra.

"I think I'm supposed to empty the apartment. We've already taken out everything of Sarah's, and mementos of her parents. I don't quite know what to do with the rest."

"Would you like me to take care of it? I know what belongs to the Army and what are their personal things. Some of the other wives and I can get together and empty the place."

Pedra felt so relieved! "Would you? That would be wonderful. I think it's difficult for Sarah to spend time here."

"We can donate or give away the extra things. If I find anything that looks official, like a will or financial documents, I'll mail them to you."

"I can see why you and Vivian were friends. You're so kind. If you incur any expense let me know and I'll reimburse you."

Chapter 17

The next morning, Pedra left the keys to the apartment with Mandy. After one more hug goodbye, Sarah turned and looked back at her old life, then took Pedra's hand and walked with her into their new adventure.

On the drive home, Pedra felt like she could be content like this, just the two of them. Maybe not ecstatic, but happy enough. She was certainly happier than she had been as a child, living alone as a young adult, or recently at the convent. Her life had meaning now that gave her a sense of accomplishment. She looked in her rearview mirror at Sarah, who had fallen asleep hugging Koko. They were going to be fine together.

She pictured Bernard and hoped he would be fine, too. She thought of him often and felt a sense of regret as she imagined what might have been. It usually helped to think of Father Frank and his example of finding gratitude for all situations.

"Thank you, God," she said aloud with no worry of waking Sarah. "Thank you that I met Frank, that I found Sarah, for the home we've been given, for the work I'll start soon that will pay enough to live simply together." She watched the scenery they passed as she drove along the road. "Thank you for the loveliness of nature, for the beauty of trees and sky and flowers. Please remind me to be grateful for what I have and not always be wanting more."

Again, Bernard came to mind, but she pushed the thought away. Then she realized he could be part of her "gratitude attitude," as well. "Thank you for Bernard. Be with him as he gets ready to start a new year teaching. Give him comfort amid the loss of his birth parents and his adoptive parents. Lead him to happiness." The prayer brought her a sense of peace.

The drive home was long, and Pedra was tired. They stopped at rest areas and restaurants and walked a bit to stretch their legs. At one of the rest areas, Sarah watched a family walking their dog. "Can I have a puppy?" she asked.

"Maybe," Pedra answered. "But let's get used to just the two of us for a while first." She wasn't sure a dog would fit into their budget, but she was tempted to give the child anything she desired. She knew that wasn't wise, but she wanted to provide every happiness she could to a little girl who had lost so much.

She was anxious to get home as soon as possible. She planned to return the rental car the next day, after they'd unloaded Sarah's things. It had been a long, long day. At last, they were almost back to Father Frank's house. *Our home*, she reframed. She turned onto their street and her heart skipped a beat to see a car very much like Bernard's parked in front of the house.

It *was* Bernard's! He was at their door, ringing the doorbell! Pedra beeped her horn. He turned and grinned as if he'd been given the best gift ever! Pedra parked in the driveway and flew into his arms. He held her in a wonderful embrace, then backed up to see her face. Sarah banged on her car window, and both hurried to release her from the booster. As soon as her shoulders were free of straps she reached out to Bernard, who enveloped her in his arms.

"I missed you! I love you!" Bernard signed to Sarah after the hug. "And your new mama" he said aloud, turning to Pedra, who was delighted that he'd learned a little sign language. He took hold of her two hands. "I've been hired by the local college to teach. I'd like to live near you two, with the hope that, once we are sure it is meant to be, we could get married and adopt Sarah together!"

Before Pedra answered, she signed what Bernard had said for Sarah to consider. The child nodded her head vigorously. Pedra turned to Bernard and added her own ecstatic head nod to Sarah's. The three hugged in a warm, comfortable unity that would remain unbroken.

The End

ABOUT THE AUTHOR

Betty Arrigotti and her husband George live near Portland, Oregon. With four daughters and eleven grandchildren, family ranks high on her priority list, above crocheting, gardening, reading, and yes, even writing.

Please visit her website at BettyArrigotti.com. She loves to hear from readers! Email her: Betty@Arrigotti.com

ALSO FROM THE AUTHOR:

Betty has written six other Contemporary Christian love stories and uses both her spiritual and counseling education to bring depth to her novels.

Hope and a Future offers marriage counseling insights as the romances unfold.

The sequel, *Where Hope Leads*, takes place in Ireland and does the same with pre-marriage counseling.

When the Vow Breaks portrays the damage that family secrets can wreak on the innocent, though grace can heal them.

Their Only Hope takes a darker turn and enters the world of human trafficking as a young man helps a young woman escape.

Miriam's Joy! asks what would happen if the Virgin Mary came to help people in your neighborhood.

Joseph's Joy follows Saint Joseph as he visits our time to help men become the best fathers and husbands possible.

Made in the USA
Middletown, DE
27 August 2024

59341124R00071